所寶惟賢　真伯文物鑒賞

# 卷三 文房雜項

# 目錄

# Contents

## Volume 3

# 明清時期皇家品味體現的文化內涵

上海大學藝術研究院副教授　胡懿勳

明清時期的宮廷用品，在繁複細緻的技術上體現皇家的品味，珍貴的材料以彰顯皇室家族的尊貴，細緻的作工則將稀有材質轉化成精美絕倫、令人讚嘆的藝術品。宮廷藝術在古代傳襲著統治階層的意志和統治地位的象徵，這些華麗尊貴的宮廷用品，表示皇家的審美品味，它們所蘊含的文化內涵，也聯繫在社會背景的脈絡之中。

## 皇家審美的脈絡

宮廷中用品製作的來源，大致由宮廷御用工匠及各地方政府進貢兩種管道。明清承襲前代的體制，完善地建立宮廷中專司生產皇家用品的機構，例如，明代織造龍袍御用織品的南京內織染局、蘇州局及杭州局，以及清初的「如意館」，將民間畫工召進宮廷為皇帝專門作畫的機構。宮廷的御用機構從事日常用品的生產，卻無法滿足皇家對於玩賞藝品的欲望，如若適逢皇家婚禮、皇家壽辰等大宴場合，則各地方政府進貢的賀禮或者皇家的陪嫁、聘禮，無不卯足全力蒐集奇珍異寶。因此，民間手工的玩賞藝品，往往也依照地方官吏揣度皇家的旨意，特別訂製而成。官方對手工業生產的掌握逐漸鬆動，使民間能工巧匠得以發揮專長，躋身皇家和文人的上層社會。

皇帝自己開發符合喜好的玩賞藝品，清代康雍乾三朝琺瑯彩瓷器可謂帝王品味的代表，帝王同時也收藏前代的精品，明代琢玉善手蘇州人陸子岡的玉器，即是清代皇宮中的重要收藏品，一九六二年北京市文物工作隊發掘清皇室墓時，發現一件玉杯，杯柄上即有「子岡」的款識。明代新安（今安徽歙縣）人，剔紅高手黃大成（字平沙，又名成），精於傳統髹漆、雕漆之法，造剔紅可媲美明代為宮廷製漆器的作坊「果園廠」，也是皇家在民間蒐集的精品。

1 葛兆光《古代中國社會與文化十講》，北京：清華大學出版社，二〇〇二年一月第一版，第四十五頁。

2 同前註

## 講求秩序的文化內涵

宮廷的審美反映出統治階層在政治思維的要求，也依循古代的傳統文化脈絡，延續講求倫理秩序，具有教化的作用。根據葛兆光先生的觀點，家族中的祠堂祭祀、家譜等型態，是古代社會生活中重要的基礎。「古代中國之所以能夠在法律並不很細緻的情況下，會有一個相對比較穩定的秩序，就是因為有這些東西在支持它，……[1]」中國古代的宗族、家族與國家體制產生了互動的關係，當國家的政治力強大時，宗族的力量可以抵消和對抗政府對百姓的直接控制。反之，國家力量衰弱，宗族「就會作為民間社會，補充國家對秩序的控制，作為社會維持生活秩序。[2]」

落實到古代宮廷文化層面而論，家庭、家族、宗族的複雜樹狀結構，形成了特有的一套宗譜、族譜的關聯，連帶著一批一批的傳家之寶、祖傳御製秘方、傳世骨董體現皇室家族的正統。原本屬於歷史、文化，間或有藝術成分的物件，經過幾代人，甚至數十代人的傳續之後，覆蓋了一層厚重的皇家血緣錦緞，一件單純的藝術品成為一個皇家重要象徵，玉器、青銅器等成為凝聚家族血緣的精神代表；工藝、繪畫名師特意為皇室製作獨一無二的藝術精品，也是贈賜官員子民的權力擴散。這些代表秩序與倫理的物件，在歷代象徵權勢的皇宮、園林裡，強化皇權的輻射。

在皇家及官員、文人的需求增加，民間藝人也在製作工藝上磨練精進，明代揚州人周翥，擅長剔紅，自創百寶嵌漆器，從大型的屏風、桌、椅、窗、格、書架，到小巧的筆床、茶具、硯匣、書箱等文房用具，精工雕琢，五色陸離，後人稱這種漆器鑲嵌作法為「周制」。明清兩代隨著嘉定、金陵、浙江三個竹雕藝術流派的興起，徽派竹雕也很快顯明於世，文房中的竹雕文玩，不但是宮廷中的貢品，同時也是當時文人們喜愛玩賞的藝品。清代蘇州人王春林，在《梵天廬叢錄》記載，清高宗南巡至無錫惠泉山，聽聞山下有王春林，善作精美之泥孩兒，便命他作泥孩兒五盤，且以錦繡、金葉裝飾，乾隆高興之餘，賜給他豐厚的金帛。

明代河北遵化、山西陽城、福建龍溪等地的銅鐵冶業，促進明代銅器製造的精良，以「宣德爐」堪稱代表。原本由官府控制的製瓷業，民窯數量逐漸超過官窯，瓷器的品質可與官瓷媲美；絲、棉等織品由於生產工具的改良，緙絲、刺繡手藝更加華麗精美，瓷器、織品都能保證皇家大量的需求。清代對元明以來匠籍制度的廢除，為私人手工業的發展提供有利條件，也促成宮廷與民間在手工藝製造技術的交流。

漢字的「道」與「一」，似乎表明，古代社會的精英與宮廷貴族、官員共同構成的上層社會階層，講求著回歸純真的精神追求，這當然與傳統文化和哲學思想密切相關。《老子》所言，「昔之得一者，天得一以清，地得一以寧，神得一以靈，穀得一以盈，萬物得一以生，侯王得一以為天下貞。」，地得一以寧，神得一以靈，穀得一初有無，無有無名」。《莊子》〈天地〉篇也說，「太易，水泉有美惡，草木有剛柔也。物得以生，謂之德；未形者有分，謂之命……」。讀書人與為官者確信簡化自我心靈，認清事物本質，方得體悟天地之間不變的真理。

從思想層面而論，宮廷貴族與知識份子體認的儒系、道家和釋家的觀念表現在精緻和文人藝術的範疇，皇家使用的食衣住行生活器用，往往在社會結構鬆動的情況之下，產生更多樣化的交換和融合。明清皇室在要求倫理秩序的前提之下，以龍紋為「象聖王應機布教也」的權力圖騰，在各種器用上表現鬼斧神工的精湛技術，構想和巧思有時也取自民間的養分。即使在技藝上稟承帝王的審美喜愛，但是在內在意涵的傳達上卻隱含民間庶民的質素。

## 反璞歸真與從樸素出發

沒有如貴族、文人般有哲學思想的開通之下，平民百姓對於技藝的承繼，又是如何的認知呢。漢代應劭在《風俗通義》自序中說，「風者，天氣有寒煖，地形有險易，水泉有美惡，草木有剛柔也。俗者，含血之類，像之而生，故言語歌謳異聲，鼓舞動作殊形，或直或邪，或善或淫也。聖人作而均齊之，咸歸於正；聖人廢，則還其本俗。[3]」應劭解釋了古代統治者對於移風易俗的教化作用，同時強調民間社會因天氣、地形、草木殊異，而形成的鼓舞動作，都是本俗的觀念，也是地域性、民族性民間藝術形式發生論的重要觀點。民間社會的布衣卻總是喜歡從「滿」出發；滿就是盈貴、充實的意思。他們在玉雕、牙骨雕、剪紙、版畫、竹木雕刻的形式上，佈滿著裝飾性的色彩、圖案、紋樣，以求豐富的視覺效果。但是，它們的心思卻是再單純也不過了，這種單純的祈願和表現，直接指向樸素的對生命延續的觀感。

古代民間藝術的表現，相當一致地從樸素出發。民間藝術向來與自我生長的土地、血緣親近，無論是戲曲、工藝等形式，也都可以直接回溯到氣候、土地、氣血這些百姓最為熟悉的養分。除去了形而上的哲學思辯，或者簡單的接受了文人主流思潮的局部影響，鄉間、市民階層的作者，對於情感的傳達是樸素而直接的。

3 應劭撰，王利器校注《風俗通義校注》北京：中華書局，一九八一年版。

中國人十分重視傳統的傳承關係。師承、血脈、宗派等等，均說明了中國人在技藝的學習獲得，都是在記憶的傳遞中開展而來。由於有了承繼傳統的觀念，許多古老的技術在新的社會中依舊使用，在已經淘汰的形式中仍然保存著。即使經過社會的動盪、戰爭的摧毀、政治的更跌，依然無法動搖傳統的根基。

從民間工匠的獨特手藝，乃至於繪畫的技法風格，書法的體式、語言與文字承襲、皇家建築樣式等等，無不可以梳理出屬於他們自身的脈絡和嬗變過程。延續傳統的文化特質中，濡化與同化的綜合作用，使得嬗變的過程漸次擴大了內容和意義，換言之，即促成了經過幾種不同文化融合的多樣性內容[4]。因而也使許多藝術的形式和內容，在不同時期的傳承中，增加與豐富了文化的性質。

## 結語

歷史的脈動，在不同時期受不同的觀念與主流意識引導，而為時代的文化與思想內容，儒系、道系、釋家各有其引領風騷的時代思想，體現在民間的庶民社會也有輕重的比重差異，或者轉化成民間所能接受的內容，讓普遍的社會大眾受其影響。過於粗糙的歸結在孔夫子高牆之內，或釋迦牟尼的空門中，都無法全面地說明中國古代藝術精神的本質。

純粹的儒家、道家或者佛家的形而上哲學思想，無法確切說明為何除了文人美術、精緻藝術、專業藝術之外，民間美術和民間各種的工藝美術型態，同樣地顯示出他們的精采樣貌，曲藝、民族舞蹈又鮮明地保有了自身的地方性、民族性色彩。只有從對生命的觀照和生活的實踐中，才能觀察中國古代人們對自身價值的認知。帝王的意志以及宮廷藝術對於民間藝人、工匠、藝伎、優人、樂師的相互影響與轉換，將高深的哲學思想融合在世俗大眾能夠感知的範圍中，體現了中國的文化特質，皇家的審美品味除了具有政治意味之外，同時也隱含濃厚的家族血緣觀照，普遍的平民百姓欣然接受恰好符合自身所受傳統觀念教導之下的這些藝術形式，可謂明清時期的宮廷藝術和民間藝術產生的互動和交流的結果。

4 文化人類學強調「文化傳播」(Diffusion)、「涵化」(Acculturation)；涵化意即文化互滲、文化適應及同化的意涵。按美國人類學家赫斯科維茨(M.J.Herskovits)的區分，「傳播是對已經完成的文化變遷的研究，而涵化則是對正在進行中的文化變遷的研究。」(《文化動力》(Cultural Dynamics)，紐約，一九六四年版，第一百七十頁)。而本文所謂之「同化」，指涉中國古代在不同文化的融合上具有涵化的事實。

Qing emperors Kangxi, Yongzheng, and Qianlong could be represented by enamel porcelain. Emperors also collected pieces from previous dynasties, and one of the most important collections of Qing Dynasty emperors was Ming Dynasty jade made by the hand of Suzhou master jade carver, Lu Zi-Gang. In 1962, when a Beijing City archeological team unearthed a Qing tomb, it discovered a jade cup whose handle bore the carved signature of Lu Zi-Gang. The Ming Dynasty's red lacquer master Huang Da-Cheng (given name also Ping-Sha or just Cheng) from Xinan (present day Shexian, Anhui Province) was highly skilled at traditional painting and carved lacquer ware. The red lacquer that he made compared favorably to that of the Guoyuan Chang which was the official lacquer ware production studio for the Ming Dynasty palace. His pieces are among the civilian made art collected by the imperial family.

As the requirements of the imperial family, officials, and literati increased, artists stepped up the hard work of improving their technical skills. The Ming Dynasty's Zhou Zhu from Yangzhou, skilled at red lacquer, invented the art of lacquer ware embedded with various treasures. Ranging from large works like screens, tables, chairs, windows, frames, or shelves to small literati study objects like brush rests, tea sets, inkstone cases, and books, the carving work was refined and fantastically colorful. After his time, people called this lacquer ware embedding method, "Zhou Zhi," after him. With the surge in popularity of the three artistic styles — Jiading, Jinling, and Zhejiang — of bamboo carving in the Ming and Qing Dynasties, the Huipai school of bamboo carving also quickly appeared. Bamboo carvings of the literati study were not only tribute gifts in the palace; they also were pieces of art that literati of the time liked to appreciate. The Qing Dynasty's Wang Chun-Lin of Suzhou was famous for clay figurines, as recorded in the official records. When Qing Emperor Qianlong traveled south to Quanshan, Wuxi, he heard that Wang Chun-Lin, who lived nearby, was skilled at making beautiful clay figurines. The emperor ordered him to make five child figurines and to decorate them with silk and gold leaf. Qianlong was so pleased that he rewarded Wang with gold and silk.

In the Ming Dynasty, the bronze production of areas such as Hebei's Zunhua, Shanxi's Yangcheng, and Fujian's Longxi boosted the excellence of that era's bronze making, epitomized by the "Xuande censer" style. Porcelain making was originally controlled by officialdom, but the number of civilian kilns gradually outstripped that of official kilns, with quality that compared favorably. The production of silk and cotton weaving and embroidery became much more gorgeous and refined because of the improvements in production tools. Porcelain and woven fabrics, therefore, could be produced in the high quantities required by the imperial family. The abandonment of the official art production system from the Yuan and Ming Dynasties provided beneficial conditions for the development of the civilian handmade art industry and boosted the exchange of handicraft techniques between the imperial court and the civilian sector.

# Cultural Connotations of the Artistic Tastes of Ming and Qing Imperial Families

Hu Yi-Hsun,
**ph. D**
**Art Research Institute of Shanghai University**

Artistic items from the palaces of the Ming and Qing Dynasties reflect the artistic tastes of the imperial families in their intricate and exquisite workmanship. Precious materials were used to express the nobility of the imperial families, and exquisite workmanship transformed these rare materials into breathtakingly gorgeous masterpieces. The arts of the palace passed on the symbols of the will, and of the ruling status of the ruling classes from ancient times. These beautiful and precious palace artworks show the aesthetic tastes of the imperial families, and the cultural connotations of these items are connected by a common thread to the social background.

## The Common Thread of Imperial Aesthetics

Artistic items in the imperial palace were basically all either manufactured by imperial artisans in the palace or presented as tribute by local governments. The Ming and Qing Dynasties carried on the system from previous dynasties, with the complete establishment of organizations within the palace that were responsible for producing certain types of art. In the Ming Dynasty, for example, the Nanjing Office of Imperial Textile Dyeing, the Suzhou Office, and the Hangzhou Office were responsible for weaving imperial robes, and, in the early Qing Dynasty, the Ruyi Guan was an organization that recruited civilian painters into the palace to paint exclusively for the emperor. The palace imperial artwork organizations worked on the production of essential everyday items, but they still could not satisfy the desires of the emperors for fancy artwork for grand occasions like imperial weddings and imperial birthdays, so the palace constantly collected fantastic artworks in the form of tribute from local governments, as well as dowries and engagement gifts. Fine ornamental artworks made by civilian artisans, therefore, were usually commissioned by local officials in consideration of the expected tastes of the imperial family. The control of officialdom over the production of handmade artworks gradually loosened, allowing civilian artisans to take their place beside the imperials and the literati in the upper levels of society.

The emperors themselves developed ornamental artworks to suit their preferences. The so-called imperial taste of intermission there was what we call the process of conferring." Scholars and office holders firmly believed in the simplification of the spirit. They understood clearly the nature of matters and correctly realized the unchanging truth of heaven and earth.

On the level of philosophy, the Confucianist, Taoist, and Buddhist concepts understood by the nobles and intellectuals of the palace were displayed in their refinement and literati art. All of the utensils and accoutrements used by the imperial family in everyday life, in the background of the loosening of social structures, produced more diverse exchanges and fusions. In Ming and Qing Dynasty palaces, on the premise of the demand for a moral order and with the dragon pattern as the totem of the emperor's authority, the finest techniques and uncanny workmanship were displayed in all the items they used, with concepts and ingenuity sometimes also deriving nourishment from the civilian sector. Even though the craftsmanship accorded with the emperors' aesthetics and preferences, there was a hidden quality that came from the common people and that was passed along in the inner meaning of these artworks.

## Cultural Connotations of Meticulous Order

The aesthetics of the palace reflect the demands of the ruling class in terms of political thought. Following the common thread of traditional culture from the ancient dynasties, the meticulous moral order was carried on, which served an educational purpose. According to  Mr. Ge Zhao-Guang, an important basis of the life of ancient society was the configuration of sacrifices and genealogies in the clan temples. "Ancient China could have relatively stable order without a detailed legal system because of the support provided by these things." [1] The clans of ancient China produced an interactive relationship with the state system. In times when the political power of the state was strong, the power of clans could counteract and resist the direct control of the common people by the government. On the other hand, when the state's power was weak, clans, "would act as a civil social organization and supplement the state's control of order, acting as the social organization that maintains everyday order." [2]

When implemented on the level of ancient palace culture, the complex tree-shaped structure of families and clans formed a set of related genealogies, bringing with it batch after batch of ancestral treasures, secret imperial art techniques, and heirlooms to manifest the ruling authority of the imperial family. After being passed down through perhaps dozens of generations, artworks that might be considered by us to belong to the realms of history, culture, or art became important symbols of the succession of power for the imperial family. Jade and bronze ware became symbolic objects in which the familial bloodline of the emperors rested. Handicraft artists and painters created unique masterpieces for the palace, so they were a means for spreading some of the palace's authority to officials and citizens. These objects that represented order and morality strengthened the radiation of imperial power from the palace and the gardens which were the historical symbols of power.

The words "dao" (the way) and "yi" (the first) basically illustrate the philosophical basis of the upper class comprised of the ruling elite, palace nobles, and officials in ancient China, and the meticulous pursuit of a return to purity. Naturally, this is closely connected to traditional culture and philosophical thought. The Dao De Jing says: "These things from ancient times arise from one: The sky is whole and clear. The earth is whole and firm. The spirit is whole and strong. The valley is whole and full. The ten thousand things are whole and alive. Kings and lords are whole, and the country is upright." The writings of Zhuang Zi say: "In the Grand Beginning (of all things) there was nothing in all the vacancy of space; there was nothing that could be named. It was in this state that there arose the first existence—the first existence, but still without bodily shape. From this, things could then be produced, (receiving) what we call their proper character. That which had no bodily shape was divided; and then without

1. Ge Zhao-Guang. Ten Talks on Ancient Chinese Society and Culture. Beijing: Tsing Hua University Press, Jan. 2002, 1st edition. 45.

2. Ibid.

allows contents and meanings to be expanded gradually in the process of evolution. In other words, the diversity of contents is promoted through the blend of different cultures.[4] This also allows the addition and enrichment of cultural qualities in the forms and contents of art forms across different periods.

## Conclusion

The pulse of history is influenced by different concepts and fashions in different periods to create the cultural and philosophical contents of each age. Confucianism, Taoism, and Buddhism all influenced the thinking of certain eras, and are all manifested in folk culture to various degrees, or were perhaps transformed into content that was acceptable to folk culture so that that the public could be influenced by them. Crude summaries of the philosophies of Confucius or Buddha, however, cannot fully explain the essence of ancient Chinese art.

Putting aside literati art, refined art, or professional art, the pure metaphysics of Confucian, Taoist, or Buddhist thought cannot accurately explain why the styles of folk art and all kinds of folk handicrafts can show their fantastic appearances. Folk art forms and racial dances also clearly preserve their own regional and racial features. Only from the perspective of the concern for life and the practice of living can we observe the recognition by ancient Chinese of their own value. For the civilian artist, artisan, performer, actor, and musician, the mutual influence and transformation with the will of the emperor and the art of the palace mixed lofty philosophical thought with the forms that the common people could understand, reflecting the characteristics of Chinese culture. Disregarding the political aspect, the aesthetic taste of the imperial families incorporated a rich concern for family heritage, and these art forms that were influenced by traditional concepts could also be easily accepted by the common people. The aesthetics of Ming and Qing Dynasty art can be called the result of the interaction and exchange between palace arts and folk arts.

4. Cultural anthropology emphasizes diffusion and acculturation. Acculturation is mutual permeation, mutual adaptation, and assimilation of cultures. According to the demarcations of American anthropologist M. J. Herskovits, "diffusion is the study of completed cultural changes, and acculturation is the study of cultural changes as they are occurring." (Cultural Dynamics. New York: 1964. 170.) The assimilation referred to in the article refers to the fact of acculturation in the blend of different cultures in ancient China.

# A Return to Simpler Times and Starting Out From Simplicity

3. Ying Shao. Feng Su Tong Yi Xiao Zhu. Beijing: Zhong Hua Shu Ju, 1981 edition.

Without the philosophical open-mindedness of the nobles and the literati, how could the common people come to understand the inheritance of artistic techniques? The Han Dynasty's Ying Shao wrote in the Feng Su Tong Yi: "Nature provides different kinds of good and bad conditions that influence common people to be good or bad. The saint is always good and correct, but when the saint is not, then he goes back to vulgar nature." [3] Ying Shao explained the educational function of ancient rulers in reforming social customs and also emphasized the concept of vulgar nature in which traditional customs are formed in civil society because of natural conditions, such as weather, terrain, and vegetation. This was an important viewpoint for understanding the genesis of regional and racial folk art styles. The commoners of civil society, however, have always preferred to start out from "fullness." Fullness means having a surplus and plentitude. Their styles of jade carving, ivory carving, paper cutting, print making, and bamboo and wood carving are full of decorative colors, pictures, and patterns in the pursuit of a rich visual effect. Their thinking was naïve, however, and the supplications and expressions born from this naivety point directly to an impression of life that extends from simplicity.

The expression of folk arts in ancient times very consistently starts out from simplicity. Folk art is always close to the land and heritage in which the artist grew up. No matter whether the form is opera or handicrafts, it always gets its nourishment directly from the things most familiar to the common people, such as climate, land, and bloodlines. Putting aside metaphysical analysis, artists from the countryside and the towns simply and directly put their emotions into their works, perhaps being influenced by the trends of the literati only in a limited way.

The Chinese people attach extreme importance to relationships of inheritance. Master-apprentice, father-son, and master-disciple relationships are examples of how artistic techniques are learned as part of the transmission of cultural memories. Using the concept of the transmission of tradition, many ancient techniques can still be used in the new society, and many ancient concepts are preserved in art forms that are no longer in use. Even social upheavals, destructive wars, and political changes cannot shake the roots of tradition.

The distinctive handicrafts of folk artisans and even the technical styles of painting, the forms of calligraphy, the transmission of language and literature, and imperial building styles cannot be organized into individual processes of evolution. In the cultural characteristics passed on as tradition, the overall function of enculturation and assimilation

# 淺談田黃奇珍

國立歷史博物館副研究員　楊式昭

## 一、以石治印的淵源

在中國印學史上，使用石材治印，一般認定是由元代的王冕啟動的[1]，因此使用石材進行刻印的起始多以王冕為界；換句話說，元代的文人開始認識到這種可以用於篆刻的美麗軟性石材。明代的文人所倡導的文人治印，使得印章的素質提升，更開啟了優質軟石進入篆刻的世界。刻印材料由銅轉為石的改變，竟然引發了一場印學史上的藝術性的新途徑，開啟了明代以後光輝燦爛的文人篆刻藝術。

明代文彭倡導的文人治印，當時所用的印章石材為何，從記載中由周亮工《印人傳》中的〈書文國博印章後〉文中，以傳聞說文彭在南京任國子監時，從一民間老翁處買得兩筐青田石的記載為最早。「見石累之，心喜之……谷中乃索其石滿百去，半以屬公，半浣公落墨。於是凍石之名，始見於世，而豔傳四方矣。」[2] 這種軟質又溫潤的石頭，能夠以筆為刀，使文人入刀簡易，並可以明顯表現刀法的特色，兼以石質溫潤、色澤美麗，因此成了文人治印的最愛。

文彭所發現的青田燈光凍石，其實早在宋代，就用作「製為文房之雅具及文人所用的印章、小件玩耍之物」明代以後，郎瑛記：「今天下盡崇處州燈明石，果溫潤可愛也。」[3] 處州是府名，隋代於永嘉置郡，而青田為其轄治之區，由於地緣的關係，處州燈明石係指今日所稱之青田石，在明代嘉靖年間已經天下盡崇，受到文人雅士的喜愛，甚至用於雕刻文房用具，或婦人裝飾。

至於壽山石的大量使用，應是在明代文彭等人以青田石刻印章之後的事。文獻記載相當少，大致說來，明朝以前田黃石通稱「黃石」，並不為世人所珍視，大約因為處州

1 劉績及朱彝尊皆有王冕使用花乳石（花藥石）治印的紀錄。見劉績《霏雪錄》欽定四庫全書，子部十。及朱彝尊（竹垞）《王冕傳》。

2 周亮工《印人傳》收錄於韓天衡編訂《歷代印人論文選》，第一百七十五頁。

3 郎瑛《七修類稿》。

4 參考方宗珪《壽山石全書》，香港八龍書屋，一九九〇年，第四十五頁。

的燈明石名揚四海，壽山石尚未為世人所知。

但自清康熙年間以後，由於壽山石進行大規模開採，品種日益豐富，壽山石佳石盡出，其中田黃石溫潤色美，特別得到清代皇族的青睞。北京故宮博物院中珍藏清代皇帝璽印中，就有不少田黃印章，如康熙帝之《戒之在得》、《七旬清健》田黃對章，乾隆帝精美的田黃《三鏈章》，都是實例。此外，咸豐帝臨終交付慈安太后的一枚田黃〈御賞〉朱文小印信，之後卻成了「辛酉政變」的歷史見證。

入清以後，田黃石被推為三坑諸石之冠，市場上身價邊增，逐漸超越其他印石，名震四海。據資料所載壽山石中的田石，價格上漲情況，委實驚人。清陳亮伯《說印》〈說田石〉文中提到他初入京時，田石價錢「每石一兩，價自六兩至十五兩而止」，以後「價至每石一兩，換銀四十餘兩。而田白一種，尤不經見」。已經是四倍以上的價錢，可見在市場上的搶手。崇彝的《說田石補》也說：「比年田黃之價，繼長增高，較諸十年前何止倍蓰。」並舉出他親眼所見的一枚雙獅鈕方體田黃印「七兩之石，竟得價二千數百元」；一枚長方六面田黃印「重不過一兩四錢，聞估人竟以二百五十元竟取之」[4]。此時的價款更是超過陳亮伯的經驗了。田石自是成了治印者、收藏家的首選。

## 二、壽山石坑

在清代康熙、雍正、乾隆年間，是壽山石雕刻的黃金時代，名手輩出，如康熙年間的楊玉璇、周尚均（周彬字尚均），治石技藝超群。同治年間的潘玉茂、林謙培，繼承楊、周的技藝，各自發展形成了「西門」與「東門」兩派，「西門」派的特色是講究刀法的圓潤，追求人物神韻的傳神描寫。「東門」派的特質，除製作印章外，更多的是利用石料的自然色澤，雕刻成人物、動物和花鳥等陳設品。

壽山石的產區，主要是分佈在福建省中部的丘陵，海拔不及千米。約在福州市的北部，與連江、羅源交界的金三角地區，以壽山村為中心，北至黨洋，南至月洋，東至連江，西至旗山，範圍僅二、三十里間。

壽山石可分為「壽山」及「月洋」兩大產區。壽山產區是壽山石的主要產區，主要山峰有高山、旗山、猴柴山、金獅公山；北面和東面還有黃巢山、柳坪和金山頂等。東邊有一條的壽山溪。這裏的田間、水際、山頭、坑洞之中，壽山石的礦藏縱橫交

5 參考方宗珪《壽山石全書》，香港八龍書屋，一九九○年，第十六頁。

錯的分佈。壽山村東南邊的加良山中有一條月洋溪，溪水匯積成月洋塘，塘邊的村落就稱為月洋村，因出產芙蓉石而名揚中外。

壽山石依產區按清代以來的分類，大致可以分為「田坑」、「水坑」和「山坑」三種，「田坑」即指壽山村壽山溪水田下砂層中所埋藏的零散獨石，這就是世間所稱的「田石」。田石無根而璞，無脈可尋，呈自然塊狀，經水流搬運到河溪沉積；多為在地的農民翻田搜掘，偶然所得，因此產量並不易預期，十分珍貴。田石按產地的不同，有上阪、中阪、下阪和碓下阪之分，以中阪田中所產田黃石的品質最佳，色濃質嫩，堪稱「田坑」之標準 5。

自清代以來，對壽山石的需求日漸殷切，開採石料的工作，從露天的揀拾，到深挖廣掘，甚至大規模的進行開採；尤以駐地官吏重兵豪奪為最。清人查慎在《壽山石歌》中，記錄了清初時鎮守福州的靖南王耿精忠，率兵對壽山進行掠奪性開採的情景：「強蕃力取如輪攻⋯⋯日役萬指千工。掘田田盡廢，鑿山山為空，崗火連三月烽，玉石俱碎汙其宮。」產地在數百年間採掘殆盡。近年因為田黃的市場價值日創新高，壽山前後的老坑，也有若干新石出現，但佳品為數不多。

## 三、田黃石的品評與分類

在清代康熙、雍正、乾隆年間，是壽山石大量問世的黃金時代，五彩繽紛的美石，硬度僅在摩氏二點五到三度之間，下刀爽利，深受明清治印的文人名家寶愛，從而豐富了知識份子的生活情趣，吸引社會上名流豪門的珍藏。因此使用者、收藏家、治印人，紛紛競相賦詩著文，以生花妙筆形容田石之美，從事賞析研究與評鑑，壽山石的分類與鑑定，也儼然成為了文人雅士的研究課題，進入了一般知識份子養成的內在規範中，成為文人生活中必備的基本知識，從而代表著高度的學養與眼界。

高兆《觀石錄》中，先將壽山石分做「水坑」、「山坑」兩個大類，又給不同石品起了種種的雅號；是屬於最早的分類。之後，毛奇齡《後觀石錄》中更進一步，進行品評壽山石，「以田坑為第一，水坑次之，山坑又次之」，從而比較科學地分定了總目。然而他們對於具體的石種，仍然是因象命名，隨色取號，評其為妙品、上品、神品等等。這在今日看來是很不科學、不知所云的。

## 四、田黃美感賞析

田黃石是壽山石中非常罕見，極其珍奇的品種。田黃石因產在田裡，色相普遍泛黃色，故稱田石，或稱田黃。田黃石產於壽山村壽山溪水田下的砂層中，「無根而璞」，無脈可尋，原始外形呈自然卵石塊狀，光嫩圓華，石質透明或半透明，溫潤可愛，肌理

田石中以田黃最為常見，田白則少見，還有色純黑或黑中帶赭者的黑田石，與色如橘皮，紅中帶赭的紅田石，都很珍貴難得。黑田石色純黑或黑中帶赭者，石質細嫩光澤，肌理的蘿蔔紋多呈流水狀，多產於下阪及鐵頭嶺一帶，有稱烏鴉皮或蛤蟆皮田石者，外有黑石皮，石多呈黃色，皮色濃淡多變，皮層厚薄不一，呈塊狀或條狀，還有一種外為黃色皮，肌理黑中帶赭，也是黑田石中的上品。至於田石中赭黃色透明的灰田石，及紅、黃、青等雜色相間的花田石，多雜質的硬田石，與田黃相似的坑頭田石，只能稱為田石的下品了。

黃皮包裹白肉的又稱「金包銀」，獨有意趣。

（二）田白：田石中白色者，多產自上、中阪，質地細膩如凝脂，微透明，其色淡白中帶嫩黃或淡青。石皮如羊脂玉般溫潤，愈往裏層，肌理愈淡，而蘿蔔紋、紅筋、格紋似鮮血絲縷愈加明顯。石品以通靈、紋細、少格者為佳，質地不遜于優質的田黃石。

（一）田黃：是田坑石中最常見的品種，產於壽山溪阪，顏色呈黃色，特點是石皮多呈微透明，肌理玲瓏清澈，且有細密清晰的蘿蔔紋。其中黃金黃、橘皮黃為上品，十分罕見；枇杷黃、桂花黃稍次；桐油黃是下品，色暗質濁。田黃中的田黃凍石，質地通靈澄澈，色如鮮蛋黃，產于壽山中阪田中，稀世罕見。還有一種「銀裹金田石」，外表黃皮包裹白色石皮，肌理呈純黃色，酷似鮮蛋，也產於中阪田，更為稀少。

直到晚清，才逐漸發展出使用產地、坑洞，來命名石種的辦法。如郭柏蒼《葭跗草堂集》和《閩產錄異》的兩部書，其中有系統的介紹了壽山石石種。在第一品類中，分為黃、白、紅、黑四色；在第二品「水坑」類中，列水晶凍、魚腦凍、天藍凍、牛角凍等名目；在第三品「山坑」類中，以產地劃分種屬，如半山、芙蓉、高山、都城坑等；同時還在每一種屬中分述細目，從而確立了以坑分種總目，以產地定石名的分類鑑定法，這種鑑定法之後為多數的壽山石鑑藏家所普遍採用，一直沿襲至今。參酌各方資料，田石大致上可以分為下列數種：

隱隱顯現細密的紋理，密而不亂，羅列有致，像剛剛出土的白蘿蔔。因為長期受到含腐蝕酸等水分浸泡，石中原本不明顯的脈絡，以格、紋的形式凸現出來。石皮外表濃艷，剖其裡，則逐漸變淡泛白，石表有時裏杏黃色或灰黑色微透明色皮，其格紋多現紅筋狀。

田黃的石雕藝術，有很多不同的技法，包括印鈕、浮雕和薄意藝術，以圓雕為主。由於受限於原石不大，多屬小型雕件。田黃石以重計價，素有「易金三倍」之說，其價值錙銖相計，兼以田石肌理凝潤，因此雕琢時連石屑也不忍有所減損。所以特別適合淺刻如畫、耗材甚微的「薄意」雕刻。這種技法的雕刻層極薄且深蘊畫意，故稱為「薄意」。

薄意作品有「黑皮田黃薄意隨型章」（圖一），黑皮田黃呈深橘色，潤澤通透，呈不規則卵形，利用外裏厚薄不均的呈水流瀉狀的黑皮，淺刻林石飛鳥，依石的濃淡變化，雜然賦形，刻工精巧雅致，是典型獨特的巧雕薄意藝術手法。「田黃辟邪獸」（圖二）為一罕見的石雕擺件。凍石色澤呈金黃色，通體凝透，石質潤澤，兼以尺寸長度達八公分，為不可多得之精品。辟邪獸頭頂蟠角長垂至背間，末端有「玉璇」款，指清康熙年間福州名手楊玉璇。楊氏風格古樸，被尊為壽山石雕鼻祖，周亮工《閩小記》及毛奇齡《後觀石錄》稱讚他的運刀之妙「如鬼工」。另一枚「田黃薄意方章」（圖三）是略呈長方形的印章，石澤金黃近橘色，六面均無瑕疵，通體半透，肌理清晰可見蘿蔔狀細紋，顏色外濃向內逐漸變淡，是田黃的標準品相；此件體型碩大，色澤鮮麗，僅在印頂飾以簡練雲紋薄意，為罕見之田黃石精品。而「田黃凍蟠虎鈕方章」（圖四）蟠虎鈕蹲坐回首，張口欲吼，肌理分明，鈕工甚精。田黃方章呈淺橘色，石質凍透，通體無瑕。印面為細朱文所刻「煙波江上」，屬書畫用閒章，為清代著名印人趙叔儒所刻，邊款「己卯三月於滬上，叔儒」，此印尺寸不大，論質材製鈕篆刻均屬精品。

此次展出印章十六件，擺件一件，俱在水準之上。本館典藏文物中亦不乏壽山石文物，大略以印章為主，僅少數壽山石雕刻。印石部分以王撫洲先生所捐贈者最精，其中頗多佳品，有清代的田黃石（圖五）色澤金黃，石質微透明，肌理玲瓏清澈，且有細密清晰的蘿蔔紋。以及田白石（圖六），黑皮田黃石雕刻薄意山水煙雲（圖七），一般田黃石的外皮多為風化含鐵的泥質物質所包裹，呈現黃色或灰黑色，此件即是呈現黑中裏黃金之美。

圖六　田白石（國立歷史博物院典藏）

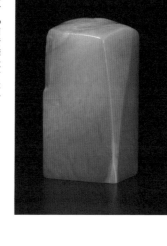

圖四　「田黃凍螭虎鈕方章」

圖三　「田黃薄意方章」

圖一　「黑皮田黃薄意隨型章」

圖七　黑皮田黃石雕刻薄意山水煙雲（國立歷史博物院典藏）

圖五　清代的田黃石（國立歷史博物院典藏）

圖二　「田黃辟邪獸」

After the reign of Qing Dynasty Emperor Kangxi (1662 – 1722), however, since Shoushan stone began to be used on a large scale, the quality improved commensurately. Because the lustrous beauty of Tianhuang stone, which was a textured Shoushan stone, attracted the attention of the Qing Dynasty imperial family, Tianhuang began to be promoted as the king of stones. The collection of Qing Dynasty imperial seals in the Palace Museum in Beijing contains many Tianhuang seals, such as Emperor Kangxi's "Jie Zhi Zai De" and "Qi Xun Qing Jian" pair of Tianhuang seals, and Emperor Qianlong's "San Lian Zhang" Tianhuang seal. Additionally, the "Yu Shang" seal given by Emperor Xianfeng, as he approached death, to Empress Dowager Ci An later became the historical evidence for the Xinchou Coup.

After the Qing Dynasty began, Tianhuang began to be promoted as the king of stones. It gradually surpassed other carving stones as its value on the market rose and its fame increased. According to the records, the rising price of field stone, the general name for this type of stone, was unbelievable. The Qing Dynasty's Chen Liang-Bo noted in "Shuo Tian Shi" from the Shuo Yin that when he first arrived in Beijing, field stone commanded, "prices from six to fifteen taels per stone," and later, "the price rose to forty taels per stone, and Tianbai stone can no longer be found." The price quadrupled on the market, which shows how hot a commodity the stone was. Chong Yi's Shuo Tian Shi Bu also says, "The price of Tianhuang continues to rise, and who can tell when it will stop climbing?" He also mentioned that he saw a double lion body Tianhuang seal that cost two hundred taels. There also was a rectangular six-sided Tianhuang seal that sold for two hundred and fifty taels.[4] The price had already risen beyond the expectations of even Chen Liang-Bo. Field stone had become the prime choice for seal makers and collectors. The time of Qing Emperors Kangxi, Yongzheng, and Qianlong (1661 – 1796) was the golden age for Shoushan stone carving, with many outstanding artists, such as Yang Yu-Xuan, Zhou Bin from the time of Kangxi, who were famed for their carving skill and were recruited into the imperial workshops to make treasures for the palace. Artisans from the reign of Emperor Tongzhi (1862 – 1874) such as Pan Yu-Mao and Lin Qian-Pei carried on the techniques of the masters Yang and Zhou, and developed the "West Gate" and "East Gate" schools. The characteristics of the West Gate school were meticulous carving techniques and smooth roundness in the pursuit of the lifelike representations of human figures. The characteristics of the East Gate school, besides the production of seals, were the use of the natural luster of stone to carve decorative human figures, animals, flowers, and birds.

4. Refer to Fang Zong-Gui. *Shoushan Stone Compendium.* Hong Kong: Balong Shuwu, 1990, pp. 45.

## 2. Shoushan Stone Quarries

The main production areas of Shoushan stone were mainly distributed in the mountainous part of central Fujian Province, with elevations that do not break 1,000 meters. In the north of Fuzhou is the "golden triangle" area, where the borders of Lianjiang and Luoyuan meet,. Centered around Shoushan Village, with Dangyang to the north,

# Brief Discussion of the Rare Treasure of Tianhuang

**Yang Shih-Chao**

**Associate Researcher**

## 1. The origins of the making of seals from stone

1. Both Liu Ji and Zhu Yi-Zun recorded that Wang Mian used huaru stone (huayao stone) to make seals. See: Liu Ji. "Fei Xue Lu". *Complete Collection of Four Treasuries*. Zibu 10; and Zhu Yi-Zun. "Zhu Cha". *Wang Mian Zhuan*.

2. Zhou Liang-Gong. *Yin Ren Zhuan*. Collected in *Li Dai Yin Ren Lun Wen Xuan* edited by Han Tian-Heng. pp. 157.

3. Lang Ying. *Qi Xiu Lei Gao*.

In the history of seals in China, it is generally agreed that using stone to make seals started with Wang Mian in the Yuan Dynasty (1271 – 1368).[1] In other words, the literati of the Yuan Dynasty had begun to understand that this beautiful soft material could be used for carving seals. It was the advocacy by Wen Peng of the Ming Dynasty (1368 – 1644) that literati should make their own seals that caused the quality of seal-making to rise and further opened the door for carving seals with high-quality soft stone. The change in seal carving material from bronze to stone actually opened up a new path in the art of seal making. It paved the way for the glorious art of seal making that followed the Ming Dynasty.

The Ming Dynasty's Wen Peng promoted the making of seals by scholars. The reason for the use of stone for making seals at that time was recorded in, "Shu Wen Guo Bo Yin Zhang Hou" in Zhou Liang-Gong's Yin Ren Zhuan. The earliest such record,[2] this states that when Wen Peng served at the Imperial Academy in Nanjing, he bought two cases of Qingtian stone from an old commoner. This type of soft and smooth stone could be carved using a brush like a knife, making it easier for scholars to carve. The special characteristics of the carving technique could be clearly expressed on the smooth and lustrous stone. It therefore, became the prefered stone for scholars making seals. The Qingtian dengguang soapstone discovered by Wen Peng had actually been used to make curios and seals of the literary studio during the Song Dynasty (960 – 1279). During the Ming Dynasty and later, Lang Ying noted the praise for the smoothness and beauty of Chuzhou dengming stone.[3] Chuzhou was a prefecture in the state of Yongjia during the Sui Dynasty (581 – 618), and Qingtian was an area under its jurisdiction. For reasons connected with geography, Chuzhou's dengming stone is what we call Qingtian stone today. During the reign of the Ming Dynasty's Jiajing (1522 – 1566), it was already famous all over China, and beloved by scholars and gentlemen of good taste. It was even used for carving literati study utensils and women's fashion ornaments.

The abundant use of Shoushan stone is probably something that happened after seals began to be made of Qingtian stone by Ming Dynasty scholars such as Wen Peng. The records are relatively sparse, but generally before the Ming Dynasty, Tianhuang stone was commonly called "yellow stone" and was not seen as especially valuable. Probably because of the fame of Chuzhou dengming stone, Shoushan stone was not well known.

described the beauty of field stone in beautiful language, and worked on the study of its evaluation and appreciation. The classification and assessment of Shoushan stone became a subject of study among scholars. It became a feature of the inner cultivation of intellectuals, a kind of essential knowledge. It thus came to represent the highest level of learning and good taste. Combining the efforts of scholars and gentlemen of good taste, Gao Zhao's Guan Shi Lu divided Shoushan stone into the two main categories of "water-mined" and "mountain-mined," and gave names to different qualities of stone. This was one of the very earliest attempts at classification. After this, Mao Qi-Ling's Hou Guan Shi Lu took the evaluation of Shoushan stone further, with field-mined stone being the best, water-mined stone the next best, followed by mountain-mined stone. This led to a more scientific cataloging of differences. They still named specific stone types, moreover, by their appearance and their color, giving them different names depending on their beauty. Today, this looks unscientific and ignorant.

By the late Qing Dynasty, the method of naming stone types by production area and excavation location had gradually developed. Examples are Guo Bo-Cang's two books, Jia Fu Cao Tang Ji, and Min Chan Lu Yi, which systematically introduced the types of Shoushan stone. In the first category are the four colors of yellow, white, red, and black. The second category was for "water-mined" stone, which had names such as Shuidong, Yunaodong, Tianlandong, and Niujiaodong. The third category was for "mountain-mined" stone, divided by production area, such as Banshan, Furong (hibiscus), Gaoshan, and Duchengkeng. At the same time, there were detailed categories within each type, which established the catalog by excavation location and the categorization and evaluation of stone names by production area. This evaluation method has since been adopted by the great majority of Shoushan stone collectors to this day.[6] After studying the available data, field stone can be roughly divided into the following types:

1) Tianhuang is the most commonly seen type of field-mined stone. It is found on the Shoushan River slopes. It has a yellow color. Its characteristics are slightly translucent stone skin with a bright and clear texture, and also a fine and distinct turnip-shape pattern. Gold yellow and orange-peel yellow are also high quality types that are very rare. Loquat yellow and osmanthus yellow are of a slightly lower quality. Tung oil yellow is an inferior quality, with a dark color and murky texture. Tianhuang soapstone, a variety of Tianhuang, has a glowing and clear texture with the color of fresh egg yolks. It is found in fields on the middle slopes of Shoushan, and is extremely rare. There is also another type of, "Silver bundle gold field stone," covered with white stone skin, with pure yellow texture, extremely similar to fresh egg yolk. It is also found in fields of the middle slopes, and is even rarer.

2) Tianbai is white field stone found both in upper and middle slopes. It has a fine texture, like congealed fat, and is slightly translucent. Its color is a pale white, with a little light yellow or pale gray. The stone skin is as smooth as suet jade, and the textures are lighter toward the inside of the stone, with a turnip-shape pattern, red veins, and a checkered pattern like bright blood silk thread that all become clearer the further one cuts into the stone. Those with

6. Refer to Fang Zong-Gui. Shoushan Stone Compendium. Hong Kong: Balong Shuwu, 1990.

Yueyang to the south, Lianjiang to the east, and Qishan to the west, its area was only about 20 by 30 li (about eight by 12 miles). Shoushan stone can be divided into the two major production areas of Shoushan and Yueyang. The Shoushan production area was the main one for Shoushan stone, and the main mountain peaks in the area include Gaoshan, Qishan, Laoling, Houchaishan, and Jinshigongshan. To the north and the south were the mountains of Huangchaoshan, Liuping, and Jinshanding. On the eastern side was the Shoushan River. The fields, streams, mountaintops, and pits of this region were crisscrossed with the mineral resources of Shoushan stone. The Yueyang River is in Jialiangshan, southeast of Shoushan Village. The river collects into the Yueyang Pond, and the village around the pond is called Yueyang Village, which is famous as the source of hibiscus stone.

Shoushan stone has been classified by production area ever since the Qing Dynasty. It can generally be divided into the three types: "field-mined," "water-mined," and "mountain-mined." The famous term, "field stone," refers to scattered individual stones buried in the sand layer of fields around Shoushan River, near Shoushan Village. Field stone is found in individual pieces in natural shapes that were transported by water to collect at the bottom of rivers. These are usually unearthed by local farmers by accident when they are tilling the earth. Production quantities are therefore unpredictable, making it very precious. Depending on the production area, field stone is divided into the categories of upper slope, middle slope, lower slope, and pestle lower slope. The Tianhuang stone found in the middle slope fields has the highest quality, with dark colors and soft texture. It is known as the standard for field-mined stone. [5]

5.Refer to Fang Zong-Gui. Shoushan Stone Compendium. Hong Kong: Balong Shuwu, 1990, pp.16.

Since the Qing Dynasty, the demand for Shoushan stone has increased, and the work of gathering the stone conducted by natural gathering and deep mining, and even large-scale excavation, usually characterized by officials and troops stationed in the local area taking the stone by force. During the early Qing Dynasty, Geng Jing-Zhong, governor of Fuzhou, led troops to Shoushan for predatory and destructive excavation, as recorded in Cha Shen's Shou Shan Shi Ge. This described how the troops destroyed the land in their large-scale efforts to take the precious stones. The production areas were mined dry after hundreds of years of work. In modern times, because of the rising price of Tianhuang stone, some old pits are still mined for the stone, but very few high quality stones can be found.

## 3. The Evaluation and Classification of Tianhuang Stone

The reigns of the Qing Dynasty Emperors Kangxi, Yongzheng, and Qianlong constitute the golden age of the popularity of Shoushan stone. It was a beautiful stone that came in many different shapes and colors, with a hardness of 2.5–3 on the Mohs scale. It was therefore, easy to carve, which made it popular with scholars, who used it to carve seals. It enriched the lives of intellectuals, and attracted wealthy collectors. Users, collectors and makers, therefore, intricate relief carvings, which are all mostly sculptures. The carvings are usually small pieces because the original stone is not big. Tianhuang stone is described as, "three times as valuable as gold," and when valued by weight, its value is measured in very small degrees. Its natural texture is also the smoothest and most beautiful of all field stones. During carving, therefore, care is taken not to waste even the slightest sliver of stone. That makes it especially suitable for shallow carving that looks like a painting, such as the intricate relief carving technique that uses up only a small amount of material. This kind of method only carves off thin layers, but still has an effect like a painting, so it is called "thin effect" in Chinese. The "Black skin Tianhuang intricate relief carving irregular shape seal" (Figure 1) is in this category. The black skin Tianhuang stone has an orange color, lustrous and translucent, in an irregular ovoid shape. It makes use of the black skin texture of different thicknesses, with intricate relief carving of trees, stones, and flying birds, with changes in shade and an unordered shape, an example of the finest carving skill. The distinctive intricate relief carving artistic technique is classic. The "Tianhuang evil-averting beast" (Figure 2) is a rare stone carving decoration. The stone's luster is a golden color. It is complete and elegant. The stone quality is lustrous. With a relatively large size, at 8cm in length, it is a rare artwork. The evil-averting beast has horns that drape from the top of its head to its back, and the end has an inscription that indicates it was made by Yang Yu-Xuan, a famous artist from Fuzhou during the reign of Kangxi. Yang had an unadorned style that respected the founders of the Shoushan stone carving style. Zhou Liang-Gong and Mao Qi-Ling both praised his carving skill as "heavenly". The "Tianhuang intricate relief carving square seal" (Figure 3) is a slightly rectangular seal with a lustrous gold, almost orange color. All six sides are flawless, complete, and semi-translucent. The texture is clear, with turnip-shaped fine lines. The color gradually turns to a darker shade from the outside to the interior. It is a standard example of Tianhuang. This piece is quite large, with a bright luster, with only a short cloud pattern carved in intricate relief on the top, a rare Tianhuang artwork. In the "Tianhuangdong dragon tiger square seal" (Figure 4), the dragon tiger sits and turn its head, with its mouth open in a roar. The texture is clearly defined and the workmanship is exquisite. It is pale orange and semi-translucent, with a complete and flawless body. The inscription says, "Yan Po Jiang Shang," which means that it was used as a poetry seal for painting and calligraphy. It was carved by the famed Qing Dynasty artisan Zhao Shu-Ru, as attributed on one side. This seal is not large, but its material, carving, and inscription are all work of the highest order. This exhibit displays 16 seals and one decoration, and they are all works of a high standard. The museum's collection does not lack for Shoushan stone, and these are mostly seals, while a small portion of them are Shoushan stone carvings. A portion of the finest seal stones was donated by Mr. Wang Fu-Zhou, such as the Qing Dynasty Tianhuang stone (Figure 5) which has a gold luster and a slight translucence. The texture is bright and clear, and there is a fine and distinct turnip-shape pattern. In the Tianbai stone (Figure 6) and the "Black skin Tianhuang stone intricate relief carving misty landscape" (Figure 7), the Tianhuang stone is generally covered by an outer skin as a result of being enveloped by ferrous muddy material, giving it a yellow or grayish black color. This item displays the beauty of gold enveloped in black.

the best stone quality are those with glowing texture, and with fine veins and less checkered patterns. The quality compares well with the best Tianhuang stone. Those with a yellow skin that covers the white stone are called, "gold covered silver," and are extremely distinctive.

The most commonly seen field stone is Tianhuang stone, and Tianbai is less commonly seen. There is also black field stone that can be pure black or black with reddish brown. Red field stone with skin like orange peel and a little reddish brown is also a rare stone. Gray field stone that is translucent with a little reddish brown and yellow, and multicolored field stone that may have red, yellow, or gray colors are mostly miscellaneous hard field stones that may be found in the same location as Tianhuang stone, though they are of a lesser quality.

## 4. The Appreciation of the Beauty of Tianhuang

Tianhuang stone is a very rare type of Shoushan stone, and it has its own rare sub-types. Tianhuang stone is found in fields, and its color is universally yellow, which gives it the name field stone or Tianhuang (field yellow) stone. Tianhuang stone is produced in the sand layer in fields around the Shoushan River, near Shoushan Village. It is scattered around, not found in a mineral vein. Its original shape is a natural ovoid stone, shiny and smooth. The stone quality is translucent or semi-translucent, smooth and attractive. The texture faintly shows some fine patterns that are distinct and orderly, like turnips that have just been unearthed. Because it has been immersed in moisture that contains corrosive acids, the originally unclear veins in the rock emerge in the form of checkers and patterns. The stone skin exterior is richly colored, but it gradually changes to pale white as it is cut towards the center. The stone surface sometimes has chestnut yellow or grayish black, slightly translucent skin, and its checkered pattern usually shows a red vein shape.

The most common field stone is yellow (Tianhuang), and white (Tianbai) is less common. There also is the rare black field stone, which can be pure black or black with reddish brown. The quality is fine and smooth, and the veins have a turnip pattern, usually with a running water shape. It is mostly produced in lower slopes and in the area around Tietouling. There is also field stone called, "crow skin," or "toad skin," that is yellow with black stone skin. The skin's color has variable shades and its thickness is variable, too. It is block shaped or stripe shaped. There is also a type with yellow skin with a black texture that has a little reddish brown. This is a higher quality type of black field stone.

There are many different kinds of Tianhuang stone carving styles. These include seal bodies, relief carvings, and

*Figure 1: "Black skin Tianhuang intricate relief carving irregular shape seal"*

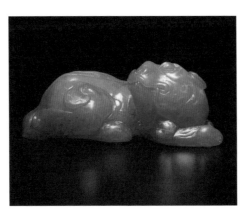

*Figure 2: "Tianhuang evil-averting beast"*

*Figure 3: "Tianhuang intricate relief carving square seal"*

*Figure 4: "Tianhuangdong dragon tiger square seal"*

*Figure 5: Qing Dynasty Tianhuang stone (Collection of National Museum of History)*

*Figure 6: Tianbai stone (Collection of National Museum of History)*

*Figure 7: Black skin Tianhuang stone intricate relief carving misty landscape (Collection of National Museum of History)*

田黃

田黃石是壽山石中非常罕見，極為珍奇的品種。田黃石產在田裡，色澤普遍泛黃色，故稱田石，或稱田黃。「田坑」即指壽山村壽山溪水田下砂層中所埋藏的零散獨石，這就是世間所稱的「田石」。田石「無根而璞」，無脈可尋，呈自然塊狀，經水流到河溪沉積，被在地的農民翻田搜掘而得，石皮外表濃艷，光嫩圓華，剖其裡則逐漸變淡泛白，石中脈絡以格、紋的形式出現紅筋，肌理玲瓏清澈，蘿蔔紋密而不亂。其中黃金黃、橘皮黃為上品，十分罕見；枇杷黃、桂花黃稍次。田黃凍石則質地通靈澄澈，色如鮮蛋黃，產于壽山中阪田中，稀世罕見。

田白多產自上、中阪，如羊脂玉般溫潤，淡白中帶嫩黃或淡青，愈往裏層，肌理愈淡，而蘿蔔紋、紅筋絲縷愈明顯，以紋細、少格者為上品。黃皮包裹白肉稱「金包銀」，及白皮包裹黃肉的「銀裏金」都少見。田石中還有色純黑或黑中帶赭的黑田石，色如橘皮、紅中帶赭的紅田石，都珍貴難得。至於赭黃色透明的灰田石，及紅、黃、青等雜色相間的花田石，多雜質的硬田石，與田黃相似的坑頭田石就只能稱為下品了。

入清以後，田黃石被推為三坑諸石之冠，市場上身價遽增，超越其他印石，名震四海。高兆《觀石錄》先將壽山石分做「水坑」、「山坑」兩個大類。之後，毛奇齡《後觀石錄》中更進一步品評壽山石：「以田坑為第一，水坑次之，山坑又次之」。自清康熙年後，壽山石佳石盡出，其中田黃石溫潤色美，特別得到清代皇族的珍愛，北京故宮博物院中珍藏清代皇帝璽印中，就有不少田黃印章。

田黃的石雕藝術，技法包括印鈕、浮雕和薄意藝術，以圓雕為主，多屬小型雕件。

田黃石以重計價，素有「易金三倍」之說，其價值錙銖相計，兼以田石肌理凝潤，麗質天生，特別適合淺刻如畫、耗材甚微的「薄意」雕刻。

國立歷史博物館副研究員

楊式昭

mostly sculptures, and they are usually small pieces. Tianhuang stone is valued by weight and is described as, "three times as valuable as gold". Its value is measured in very small degrees. Tianhuang stone's texture is smooth and naturally beautiful, so it is especially suitable for shallow carving that looks like a painting, such as the intricate relief carving technique that uses up only a small amount of material.

**Yang Shih-Chao**
**Associate Researcher**

# Tianhuang　Loose Natural Jade Not Found in a Vein

Tianhuang stone, the rarest type of Shoushan stone, is an extremely treasured variety. Tianhuang stone is found in fields and its luster is mostly yellow, thus providing its name as field stone or Tianhuang ("field yellow"). "Field-mined" refers to scattered individual stones buried in the sand layer of fields around Shoushan River near Shoushan Village, and this is what the world calls "field stone". Field stone is "loose natural jade" that does not lie in a mineral vein in the earth and is naturally shaped in pieces. It flows with the water into the river deposits and is discovered by local farmers when they are tilling the soil. The stone skin exterior is richly colored, shiny and smooth, and gradually changes to pale white as it is cut towards the center. The texture inside the stone shows red veins in checkered patterns. The texture is bright and clear, with a fine, but not disordered, turnip-shaped pattern. Gold yellow and orange-peel yellow are also high-quality types that are very rare. Loquat yellow and osmanthus yellow are of a slightly lower quality. Tianhuang soapstone has a glowing and clear texture with the color of fresh egg yolks. It is found in fields on the middle slopes of Shoushan, and is extremely rare.

Tianbai is found both in upper and middle slopes. It is smooth as suet jade and its color is a pale white with a little light yellow or pale gray. The textures are lighter toward the inside of the stone, with a turnip-shape pattern and fine red veins. Those with a finer pattern and fewer checkers represent the finest quality. Those with yellow skin that covers the white stone are called, "gold covered silver," and those with white skin that covers yellow stone are called, "silver bundle gold", and both are rare. There is also black field stone that can be pure black or black with reddish brown. Red field stone with skin like orange peel and a little reddish brown is also a rare stone. Gray field stone that is translucent with a little reddish brown and yellow, and multicolored field stone that may have red, yellow, or gray colors are mostly miscellaneous hard field stones that may be found in the same location as Tianhuang stone, though they are of lesser quality.

After the Ch'ing Dynasty began, Tianhuang began to be promoted as the king of stones. It gradually surpassed other carving stones as its value on the market rose and its fame increased. Gao Zhao's Guan Shi Lu divided Shoushan stone into the two main categories of, "water-mined," and, "mountain-mined". After this, Mao Qi-Ling's Hou Guan Shi Lu took the evaluation of Shoushan stone further, with field-mined stone being the best, followed by water-mined stone and then mountain-mined stone. After the time of Ch'ing Dynasty Emperor Kangxi, the lustrous beauty of Tianhuang stone, which was a textured Shoushan stone, was especially loved by the Ch'ing Dynasty imperial family. The collection of Ch'ing Dynasty imperial seals in the Palace Museum in Beijing contains many Tianhuang seals.

Tianhuang stone carving techniques include seal bodies, relief carvings, and intricate relief carvings, which are all

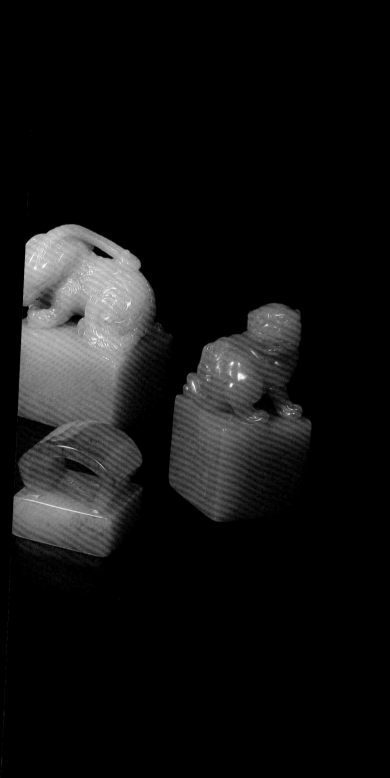

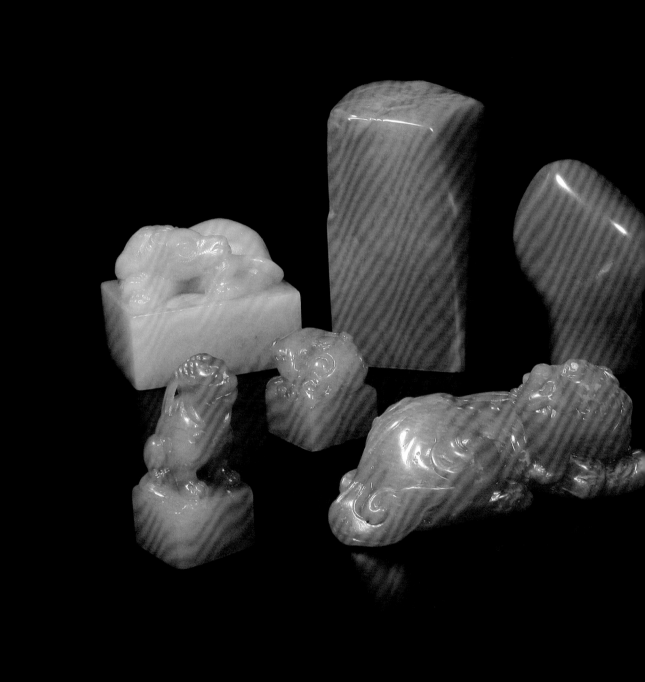

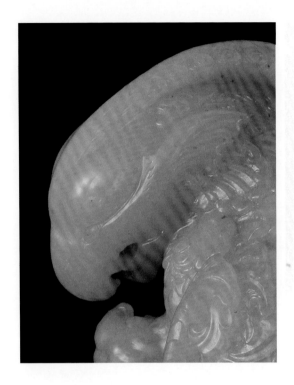

# 清　田黃　獸鈕方章

長4公分　寬3.3公分　高5.4公分　123公克

田黃方章，上有獸鈕，獸形怪異，為鷹首鉤喙長垂角獸身，張口欲鳴。印石色澤呈黃橘色，至鈕首石色漸次減淡，合乎田黃石在石皮外表濃艷，剖其裡則逐漸變淡泛白的一般特徵。印面為「皇子書印」。

*Qing Dynasty*
***Tianhuang beast body square seal***
***Inscription: Huang Zi Shu Yin***

*L/4cm, W/3.3cm, H/5.4cm　123g*

*Tianhuang square seal with beast body. The beast's shape is unusual, with an eagle head and hooked beak with long hanging horns and a beast body. The mouth is open in a scream. The stone is yellowish orange, with the color fading at the top. The stone is darker on the outside, but it reveals lighter stone on the inside, a characteristic of Tianhuang stone. The inscription reads "Huang Zi Shu Yin".*

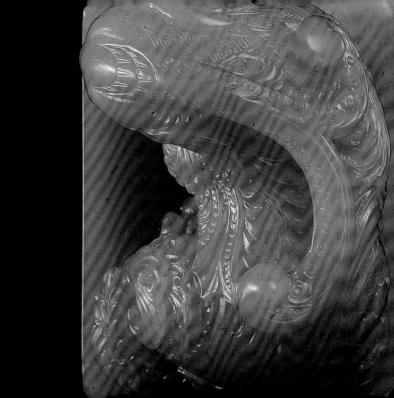

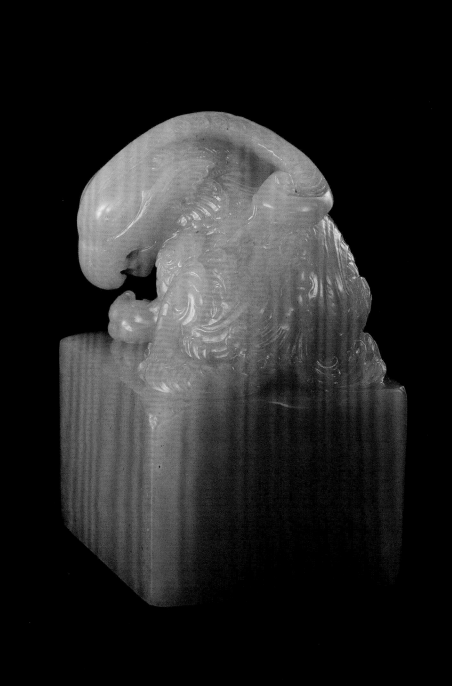

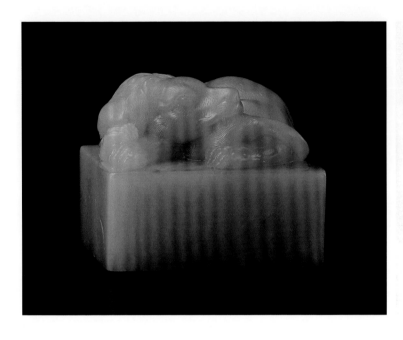

## 清　田黃　獸鈕方章

長5.5公分　寬4.3公分　高4.4公分　194公克

田白印章，雙獸紋印鈕，刻一伏獸疊足蜷臥，首尾相接。印石色澤淡黃，溫潤有如凝脂。印面刻「樂善堂圖書記」，屬璽印中之藏書印。

*Qing Dynasty*
*Tianhuang beast body square seal*
*Inscription: Le Yi Tang Tu Shu Ji*

*L/5.5cm, W/4.3cm, H/4.4cm　194ag*

*Tianbai seal with double beast pattern body, carved with curled up beasts with heads and tails connected. The stone's luster is light yellow, like congealed fat. The inscription is "Le Shan Tang Tu Shu Ji", making it an imperial book collection seal.*

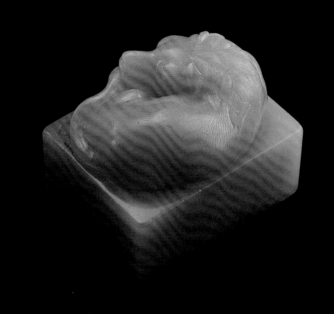

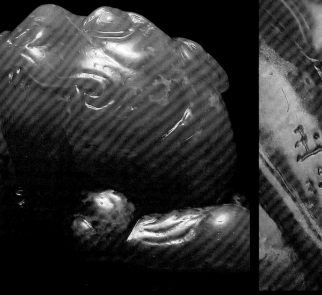
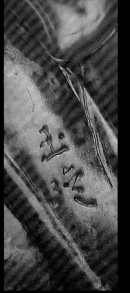

# Qing Dynasty
## *Tianhuang evil-averting beast paperweight*
## *Yu Xuan signature*

*L/8cm, W/5cm, H/3.5cm    159g*

*Tianhuang soapstone paperweight, carved into an evil-averting beast with a turned head and curled tail. The horns on the top of the evil-averting beast's head trail down its back, and the base has the "Yu Xuan" signature, indicating it was created by the master Yang Yu-Xuan, who lived in Fuzhou during the reign of Qing Emperor Kangxi. Master Yang carved many Tianhuang seal bodies and human figures with a simple and unsophisticated style. He has been called the founder of Shoushan stone carving, and his work was praised as "magical" by his contemporaries. The stone's luster is a golden color. It is complete and elegant. The stone quality is lustrous. With relatively large size, at 8cm in length, it is a rare artwork.*

清 田黃 辟邪獸書鎮 玉璇款

長8公分　寬5公分　高3.5公分　159公克

田黃凍石書鎮，刻一辟邪獸伏臥，回首蜷尾。辟邪獸頭頂頂螭角長垂至背間，末端有「玉璇」款，考為清康熙年間福州名手楊玉璇。楊氏刻製不少田黃印鈕及人物作品，風格古樸，被尊為壽山石雕鼻祖，周亮工《閩小記》及毛奇齡《後觀石錄》稱讚他的運刀之妙「如鬼工」。凍石色澤呈橘黃色，通體通透，石質潤澤，兼以尺寸較大，長度達八公分，為不可多得之精品。

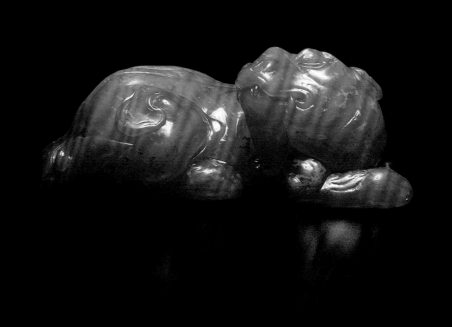

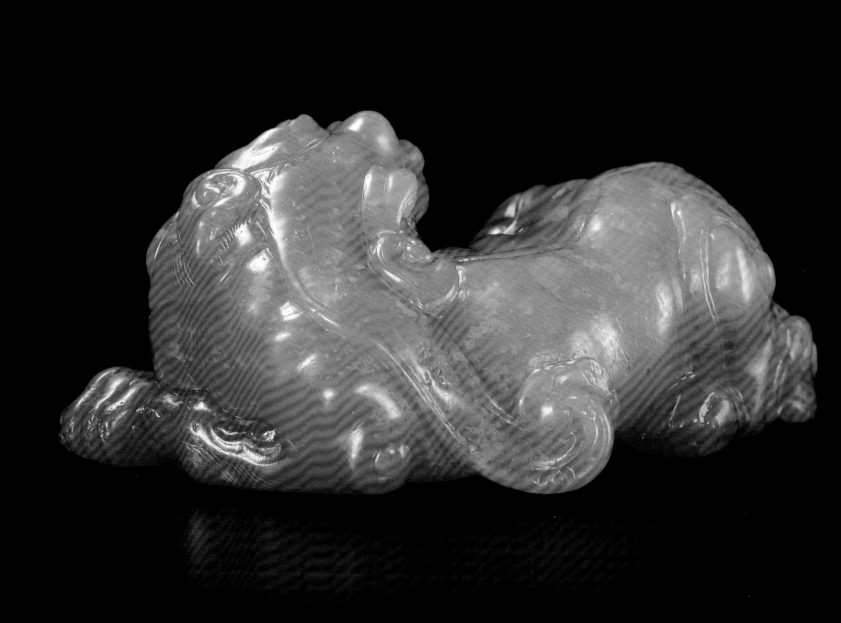

# 清　田黃　螭虎鈕方章

長2.6公分　寬2.6公分　高5.3公分　62公克

田黃凍石方章，上刻螭虎鈕，螭虎蹲坐回首，張口欲吼，肌理層次分明，鈕工甚精。田黃方章呈淺橘色，石質凍透，通體無瑕。印面為細朱文所刻「煙波江上」，屬書畫用閒章，為清代著名印人趙叔儒所刻，尚留有邊款：「己卯三月於滬上，叔儒」。

**Qing Dynasty**
*Tianhuangdong dragon tiger square seal*
*Inscription: Yan Po Jiang Shang*

*L/2.6cm, W/2.6cm, H/5.3cm　　62g*

*Tianhuang soapstone square seal carved into a dragon tiger body. The dragon tiger sits and turns its head, with its mouth open in a roar. The texture has clearly defined layers and the workmanship is exquisite. It is pale orange and semi-translucent, with a complete and flawless body. The inscription says, "Yan Po Jiang Shang," which means it was used as a poetry seal for painting and calligraphy. It was carved by the famed Qing Dynasty artisan Zhao Shu-Ru, as indicated by the attribution on one of its sides.*

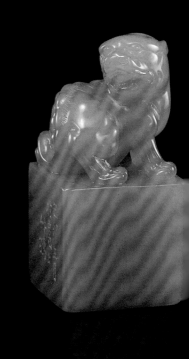

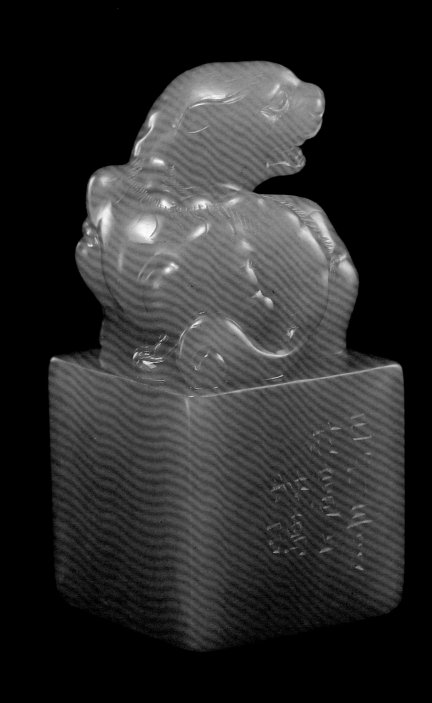

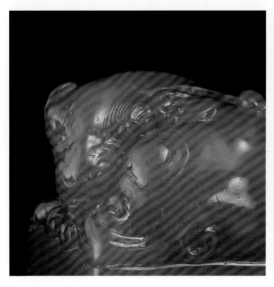 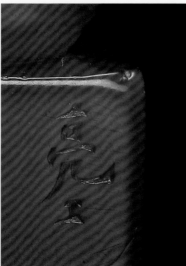 

## 清　田黃　辟邪鈕方章

長2.4公分　寬2.4公分　高2.4公分　32公克

田黃方章，上刻辟邪鈕，刻辟邪獸伏臥狀。田黃色澤鮮黃，呈半透明，肌理隱現蘿蔔紋。印面刻朱文：「風流日長」，側署「亮工」楷書，為治印者款識。

### Qing Dynasty
### *Tianhuang evil-averting body square seal*

*L/2.4cm, W/2.4cm, H/2.4cm　32g*

*Tianhuang square seal with body carved into a reclining evil-averting beast. The Tianhuang is a lustrous yellow, and semi-translucent, with a texture that subtly reveals a turnip-shaped pattern. The inscription reads "Feng Liu Ri Chang", and the side says "Liang Gong" in regular script, which is the trademark of the artisan.*

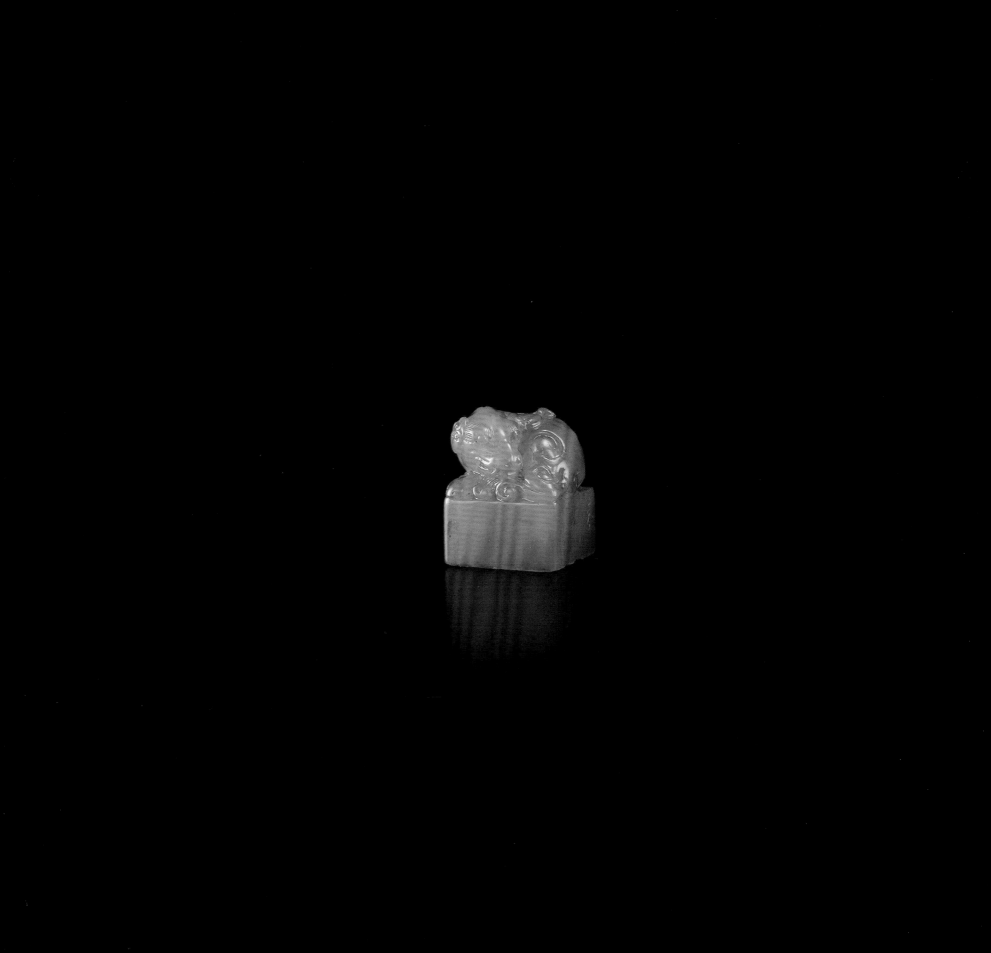

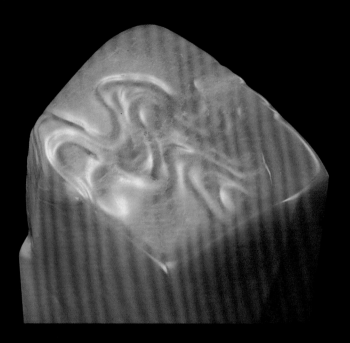

## *Qing Dynasty*
### *Tianhuang intricate relief carving square seal*

*L/4.4cm, W/3.2cm, H/8.4cm    290g*

*Tianhuang soapstone seal, slightly rectangular, with a lustrous gold, almost orange color. All six sides are flawless, complete, and semi-translucent. The texture is clear, with turnip-shaped fine lines. The color gradually turns to a darker shade from the outside to the interior. It is a standard example of Tianhuang. This piece is quite large, with a bright luster, a rare Tianhuang artwork. This seal is outstanding merely for its material, with only a slight carving on the top, and no characters inscribed on the bottom.*

田黃凍石印章，此印略呈長方形，色澤金黃近橘色，六面均無瑕疵，通體半透明，肌理清晰可見蘿蔔狀細紋，顏色外濃向內逐漸變淡，是田黃的標準品相。此件體型碩大，色澤鮮麗，為不可多得之田黃石精品。此印以質材取勝，僅見印頂簡練雲紋作為鈕飾，亦未刻印面。

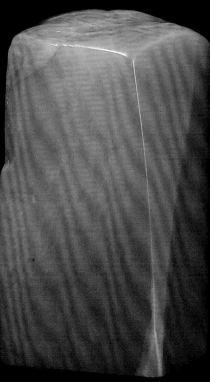

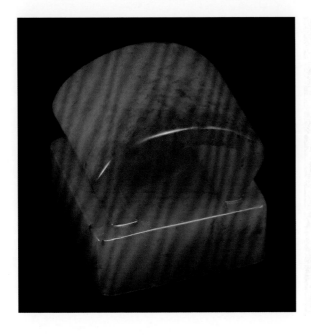

## Qing Dynasty
### *Tianhuang tile body square seal*

*L/2.5cm, W/2.5cm, H/2.5cm　24g*

*Tianhuang square seal with tile-shaped body. The carving work is succinct. The stone quality is almost orange, and is bright and translucent, with a clear, turnip-shaped pattern. It is extremely rare and known also as weihongtian stone. The inscription says "Ren He Zhu Shi Zhen Cang" which makes it a collection seal, with no signature of the artisan.*

# 清　田黃　瓦鈕方章

長2.5公分　寬2.5公分　高2.5公分　24公克

田黃方章，上為瓦鈕，刀工簡練。田黃石質近橘色，鮮豔通明，蘿蔔紋理清晰可見，或有稱作煨紅田者，十分難能可貴。印面以細朱文「仁和朱氏珍藏」六字印，係收藏章，無款。

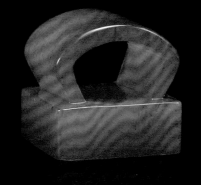

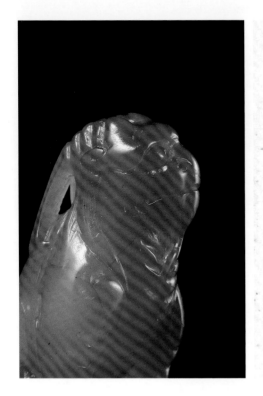

**Qing Dynasty**
**Tianhuang evil-averting body square seal**

*L/2.2cm, W/2.2cm, H/4.7cm　32g*

*Tianhuang square seal with a body carved into a crouching, evil-averting beast with one protruding eye and trailing, long horns. The seal is a lustrous dark yellow, and slightly translucent. The inscription says "Hai Feng Bi Yun."*

# 清　田黃　辟邪鈕方章

長2.2公分　寬2.2公分　高4.7公分　32公克

田黃方章，上刻辟邪鈕，刻一蹲坐凸睛垂長角之辟邪獸。此印色澤深黃，呈微透明狀，印文刻「海風碧雲」。

# 清　田黃　辟邪鈕方章

長1.8公分　寬1.7公分　高2.6公分　15公克

田黃方章，上刻辟邪鈕，刻一大眼凸睛垂長角之辟邪獸伏踞回首。田黃方章色澤金黃，微現蘿蔔紋。

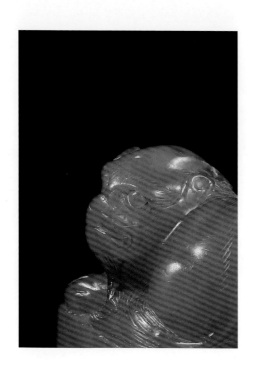

### Qing Dynasty
### Tianhuang evil-averting body square seal

*L/1.8cm, W/1.7cm, H/2.6cm　15g*

*Tianhuang square seal, with a body carved into a crouching, evil-averting beast with one protruding eye and trailing long horns, turning its head. The Tianhuang is a lustrous golden color, with a slight, turnip-shaped pattern.*

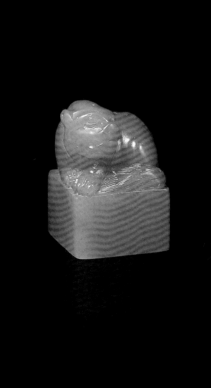

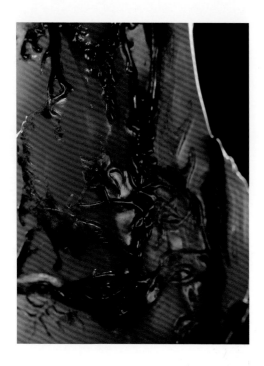

# 清　黑皮田黃　薄意隨型章

寬3.5公分　高5.7公分　52公克

田黃凍石印章，上見黑色皮質呈水流瀉狀，即是世間所稱之「黑皮田黃」者也，又稱「蛤蟆皮田黃」。田黃凍石呈深橘色，潤澤通透，呈不規則卵形，利用外裹厚薄不均的黑皮，巧雕薄意，刻林石飛鳥，濃淡變化，雜然賦形，刻工精巧雅致。

亦有稱之為「烏鴉皮田黃」

## Qing Dynasty
### *Black skin Tianhuang intricate relief carving irregular shape seal*

*W/3.5cm, H/5.7cm　52g*

*Tianhuang soapstone seal, with a black skinlike texture like trickling water. This is what is called "Black Skin Tianhuang," known also as "Crow Skin Tianhuang" and "Toad Skin Tianhuang." The Tianghuang stone has an orange color, lustrous and translucent, in an irregular ovoid shape. It makes use of the black skin texture of different thicknesses, with intricate relief carving of trees, stones, and flying birds, with changes in shade and an unordered shape, an example of the finest carving skill.*

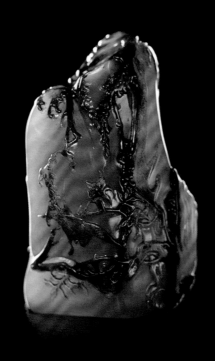

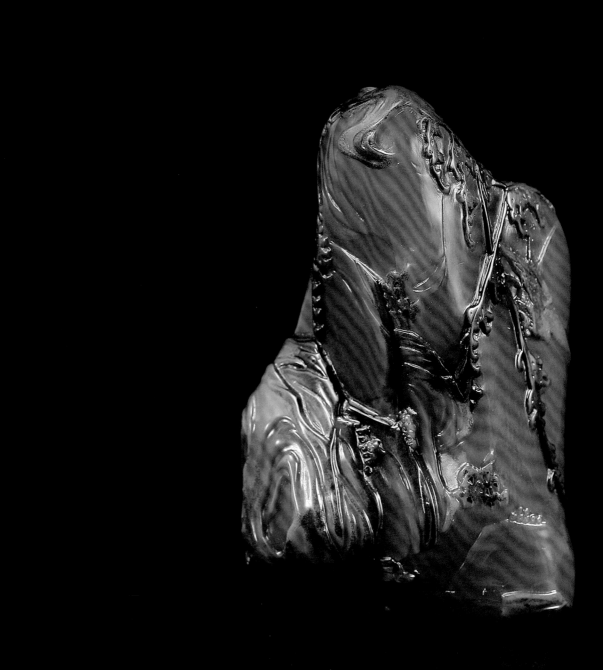

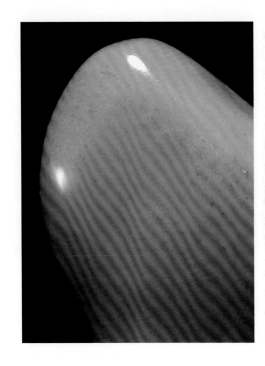 

# 清　田黃　隨形章

高6.2公分　122公克

田黃石印章，色澤金黃，尚保留石頭原始不規則卵形，通體樸素無紋飾，一面略見石之紋路，印文：「但恨貧分學」朱文印。

**Qing Dynasty**
*Tianhuang natural shape seal*

*H/6.2cm　122g*

*Tianhuang stone steal in lustrous gold, the top part retaining the original irregular ovoid shape of the stone. It is complete, simple, and unadorned. The stone's veins can be seen on one side. Inscription: "Dan Hen Pin Fen Xue."*

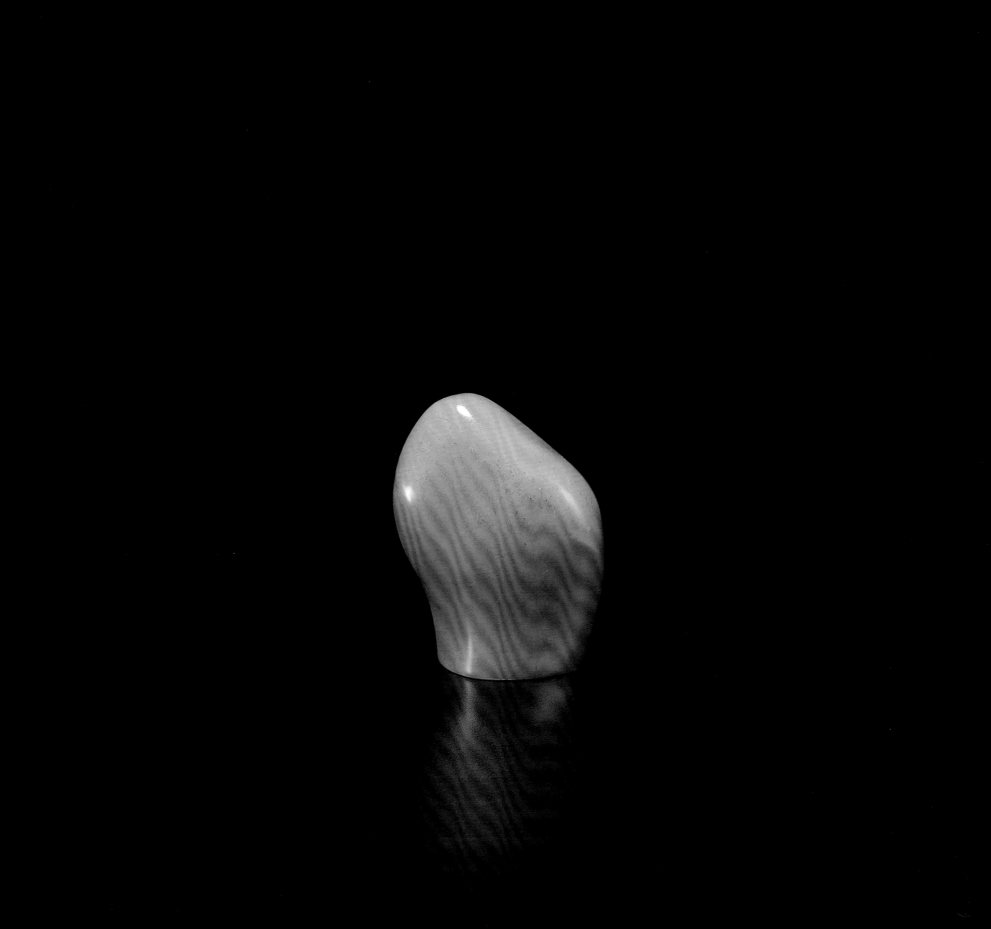

**Qing Dynasty**
**White hibiscus square seal**
**Shang Jun signature**

*L/3.5cm，W/2.6cm，H/5.1cm*

White hibiscus square seal—rectangular bar seal. The top is a flat body, with a double hornless dragon decoration in light relief. There is a double phoenix pattern carved all the way around the top part of the seal, with a "Shang Jun" signature, which may mean it is the work of Zhou Bin, a master from the reign of Qing Dynasty Emperor Kangxi. His style, which was magnificent and exuberant, bold and exaggerated, was called the, "Shang Jun seal body style." The stone quality is clean, white like congealed fat. There is no inscription.

# 清　白芙蓉石　方章

長3.5公分　寬2.6公分　高5.1公分

白芙蓉方章，長方形條印。上為平鈕，頂以淺雕雙螭紋為飾，印章上端四面各刻飾以雙鸞紋飾帶一匝。有「尚均」款，可能為清康熙時製鈕名手周彬，風格華茂兼具，大膽誇張，藝界稱之為「尚均鈕」。石質乾淨，白如凝脂，未刻印面。

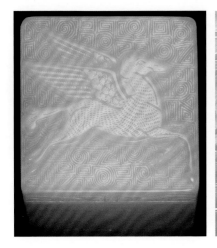  

清　白芙蓉石　平鈕飛馬紋方章

長2.5公分　寬2.5公分　高6.3公分

白芙蓉方章，上為平鈕，頂以淺雕飛馬紋飾，有「尚均」款，考為清康熙時製鈕名手周彬，風格華茂兼具，大膽誇張，藝界稱之為「尚均鈕」。印章面文為「張嘉蔭」，姓名印，屬陰文仿漢印風格，無刻印邊款。

*Qing Dynasty*
*White hibiscus flat body flying horse pattern square seal*
*Inscription: Zhang Jia Yin*

*L/2.5cm, W/2.5cm, H/6.3cm*

*White hibiscus square seal. The top is a flat body, with a flying horse decoration in light relief, with a "Shang Jun" signature, which makes it the work of Zhou Bin, a master from the reign of Qing Dynasty Emperor Kangxi. His style, which was magnificent and exuberant, bold and exaggerated, was called the "Shang Jun seal body style." The inscription says, "Zhang Jia Yin," so it is a name seal, modeled after the Han Dynasty seal style. There is no inscription on the side.*

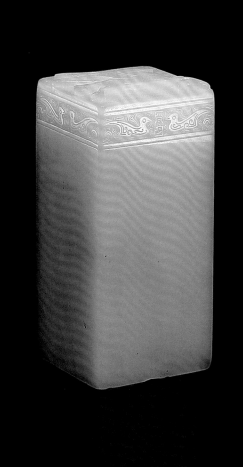

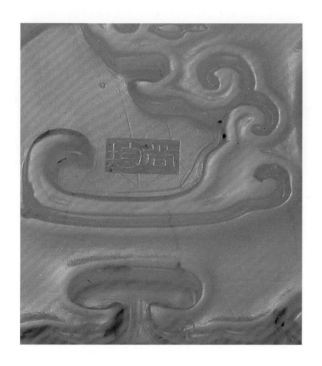

**Qing Dynasty**
**Hibiscus flat top flying bird pattern square seal**

*L/2.2cm, W/2.2cm, H/5.8cm*

*Shoushan white hibiscus stone seal—with a flying bird pattern on the body. All four sides of the seal have intricate relief carving of double hornless dragon with intertwined necks, making it extremely fancy. The stone quality is pure, with slight veins, and the stone bears a "Shang Jun" signature. There is no inscription.*

清　芙蓉石　平頂飛鳥紋方章

長2.2公分　寬2.2公分　高5.8公分

壽山白芙蓉石章，上為飛鳥紋平鈕，印章四面上端以薄意淺雕雙螭交頸，頗富雅趣。石質淨透，略現石紋。有「尚均」款，未刻印面。

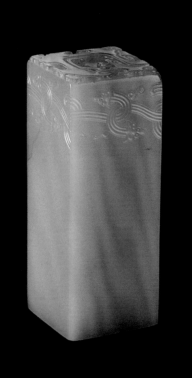

# 清　杜陵石　平頂方對章

長2.2公分　寬2.2公分　高7.3公分

壽山杜陵坑石印，為對章。印面一為陰文「李念仔印」，一為陽文「德澤」，為姓名印。此對章尺寸成對，石質淺黃，潤澤勻淨，為壽山石中杜陵坑佳品。

## Qing Dynasty
## Duling stone flat top pair of square seals

*L/2.2cm, W/2.2cm, H/7.3cm*

Shoushan Dulin stone. A pair of seals. One of the inscriptions says "Li Nian Zai Yin" and the other one says "De Ze", so they are name seals. The sizes match, and the stone quality is light yellow, lustrous, and pure, making them excellent pieces of Shoushan stone from the Dulin quarry.

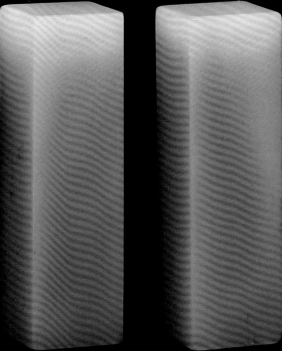

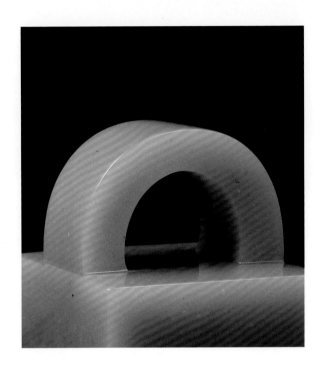

長5公分　寬5公分　高4.8公分　155公克

# 清　青田石　瓦鈕方章

青田石章，上有瓦形鈕，切工方整，樸素無紋。石呈濃黃色，微透青意，通體無瑕，未刻印面。

**Qing Dynasty**
**Qingtian tile body square seal**

*L/5cm, W/5cm, H/4.8cm　155g*

*Qingtian stone seal—with a body shaped like a tile, with a carving technique that is perfect, simple, and unadorned.*
*The stone is dark yellow, with a slight green to it. It is complete and flawless, and has no inscription.*

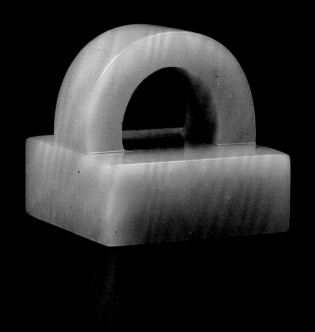

# 犀角

屖角文叫「奴色」，是長在犀牛頭蓋骨的綱生物，因為此物有凹下去的構造，而呈現圓錐的形狀，所以有人將之當作飲器，也有人用來作為裝飾品，如帶、簪等等。對中國人而言，犀角更為珍貴之處，在於其具有「清熱解毒」的效果，變成珍貴藥材之一。殷商的甲骨文中有「獵犀獲犀」的記載。古人把犀牛視為國之寶，將犀角與夜光璧、明月珠以及金銀奇寶相提並論。《韓詩外傳》載：「太公使南宮適至義渠，得駭雞犀以獻紂。」《抱樸子·登陟》中記有：「通天犀其角一尺以上，刻為魚而銜以入水，水常為開。」雖是傳說，但足說明犀角貴重。

從明代開始，犀角雕刻進入迅速發展時期，能工巧匠各顯其能，根據犀角特有的造型姿態，表面的紋理，精雕細琢成一件件奇巧精美的杯、盒、扇墜、髮簪與印章等，犀角雕刻與竹、木、金、玉的雕刻藝術，都被視為藝林珍賞之品，其中以犀角杯最負盛名。《格古要論》記載，明代以來江蘇一帶犀角雕刻工藝逐漸興起，其中著名的犀角雕刻大師有鮑天成、濮仲謙、尤通和尚等等，他們雕刻的犀角杯設計奇巧，工細絕倫，是當時世人追捧的藝術珍品。

在乾隆皇帝在位期間，犀角杯的收藏，成了一時的風尚。清朝的犀角杯，在雕刻工藝上更為精細、考究，在杯身所刻題材紋飾上講究頗多，各成體系，鍾情山水清潤，詩境古韻，便在杯身雕繪碧波松石，蕩舟垂釣，閒暇豁達的情境躍然其上。犀角杯歷經幾百年繁盛，在圖案的構成上，注重運用疏密、繁簡、動靜，大小及深淺的對比，圖案式表現手法，既有典型的蟠螭、獸面、幾何紋，也有雲水、龍鳳紋，刻畫物件更加主次分明，形象生動，線條流暢，整體感更為強烈。

從明代到晚清，數百年間，犀角杯由簡而繁，經歷了由質樸到奢華，再到對藝術境界的捕提與探尋的蛻變，不僅是工藝師手中雕刻出的藝術靈感，更是犀角雕刻藝術的發展歷程。犀角雕刻是實用和藝術的完美結合，工匠們的技巧，無論是利用深雕、淺雕、鏤空雕等，都是要讓杯上紋飾有著各自不同的意境；巧妙地利用犀角的材質，和犀角所特有的質感的扭曲、虯勁等特徵，再敷以雕琢山水、松石，意境幽遠。如今，珍貴的材質，精美的雕工，充滿深意的文化內涵，使得犀角杯成為牙角類古玩中的精品，在工藝藝術上有著特殊的地位。

國立歷史博物館研究人員

蔡耀慶

beauty. The artists wanted to make the decorations on the cup display different atmospheres, whether they used deep relief, shallow relief, or piercing carving. They cleverly used the material and texture of the rhino horn, as well as its characteristics of curviness and sturdiness, to carve it into landscapes, pines and rocks, or poetic dreamlands. Today, the rare material, fine carving work, and abundant cultural significance of rhino horn cups give them a special status among finely crafted artifacts.

**Tsai Yao-Ching**

**Assistant,**
**National Museum of History**

Rhino horn comes from the bone-covered protuberance on the heads of rhinoceroses, formed by hair and keratose. Because this object has a concave structure, it forms into a cone shape. Some people have therefore, used it for a drinking vessel, and some use it as a decoration, such as on belts and hairpins. For Chinese, the valuable aspect of rhino horn is in its medicinal effect. The oracle bones of the Yin-Shang Dynasty (1600 BC – 1100 BC) record the hunting of rhinos for their horns. Ancient people saw rhino horn as a national treasure, and compared it to jade and pearls. Poetry from the Western Han Dynasty (206 BC – 24 AD) said that horn from a mythical rhino-like beast was acquired for tribute from the kingdom of Yiqu. A text from the Eastern Jin Dynasty (316 – 420) said that the horn from this beast would cause water to boil when immersed. Although these are legends, it shows how much importance was attached to rhino horn.

In the Ming Dynasty, rhino horn carving entered a stage of rapid development, and many skilled artisans displayed their talents. They used the special shape and characteristics of rhino horn to intricately carve gorgeous cups, boxes, fan handles, hairpins, and seals. Along with bamboo, wood, gold, and jade carvings, rhino carvings were considered valuable artworks, of which rhino horn cups were the most famous. It can be seen from the literature of the time that, since the Ming Dynasty, the art of rhino horn carving gradually became prominent in the Jiangsu region. Famous rhino horn carving artists included Bao Tian-Cheng, Pu Zhong-Qian, and the monk You Tong. The designs of their rhino horn cups were clever, and the work exquisite, making them masterpieces that were highly sought after in their time.

During the reign of Qing Emperor Qianlong, collecting rhino horn cups was fashionable. Qing Dynasty rhino horn cups were particularly exquisite and meticulous in terms of carving workmanship. There were many schools, and some preferred landscape scenes, while others preferred subjects from poetry. The art of rhino horn cups flourished for centuries. In terms of composition, emphasis was placed on using contrasts, such as between complexity and simplicity. There were classic patterns, like hornless dragons, beast faces, and geometric designs, as well as clouds and water and dragons and phoenixes. Emphasis was placed on a main subject contrasted with a background to create lively images and flowing lines and to intensify the overall feeling.

In the centuries between the Ming Dynasty and the late Qing Dynasty, rhino horn cup designs went from simple to complex and from down-to-earth to luxurious. They were also transformed into an art form that pursued the highest artistic ambitions. This was not just because of the personal inspirations of the rhino horn artists. It was part of the overall course of development of the art of carving. Rhino horn carving is the ultimate combination of practicality and

## Ming Dynasty
### Rhino horn carving Guanyin seated statue

*W/15cm, H/13.5cm*

*This Guanyin Buddhist statue is carved in sculpture form, carved deep at the top and shallow at the bottom, with an ancient-looking chestnut color. There is a substantial luster with a shining brown surface that is a little red, as if there were a layer of brightness inside. After many years of handling, the rhino horn's luster has become more and more solid. There are many styles of Guanyin statues, and this one sits on one leg with a solemn expression, transcending the world of emotions.*

觀音法相以圓雕技法製，上深下淺，呈古栗色。色澤深沉，光亮的表面褐色中微微泛紅，好似包有一層亮漿，經過長時間的把玩，犀角自然的色澤變得更加厚重。觀音有多種形象，此座觀音一腳趺坐，神情靜定，宛如解脫世情六慾、超越喜怒哀樂。

# 明　犀角　豆莢小杯

長8.1公分　高2.5公分

以犀角雕成枝梗苞葉，構思巧妙，造型生動，刀法粗獷有力、樸拙厚重而不失精巧，杯身上刻繪的紋飾是高浮雕的，在杯柄處還有鏤空的枝幹，自然而實用，又在不經意中流露出犀角潤澤的質感。從整體看去，杯身造型瑰麗中充滿動感，精湛的雕刻工藝遵循犀角自然的形態，除了運用深淺浮雕外，並無過多的鏤空修飾，整只犀角杯於雄渾中透露著奇險，其內涵和工藝都難得一見。

***Ming Dynasty***
***Rhino horn carving bean pod small cup***

*L/8.1cm, H/2.5cm*

*The rhino horn is carved into a bean pod in an example of clever conception and lifelike form. Its shape is substantial, while retaining its refinement. This cup is carved with patterns in high relief, and the handle is a stem with a hole, making it natural-looking and useful. It seems to reveal the beauty of the material's luster almost effortlessly. Looking at the piece as a whole, the beautiful shape of the cup is quite moving and the intricate carving technique follows the natural state of the rhino horn. Except for the use of deep and shallow relief carving, there is not an excess of ornamental carving, making the entire rhino horn cup reveal just a little intricacy in the midst of its boldness. It is a rare piece, rich in artistic significance and fine workmanship.*

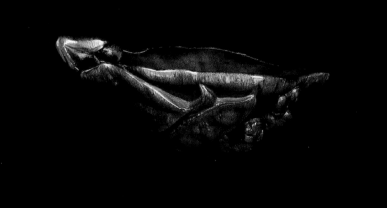

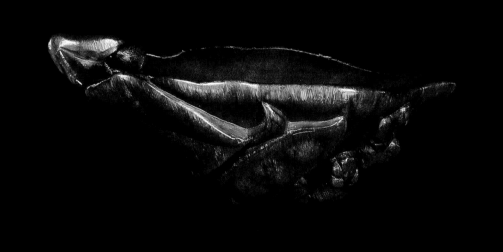

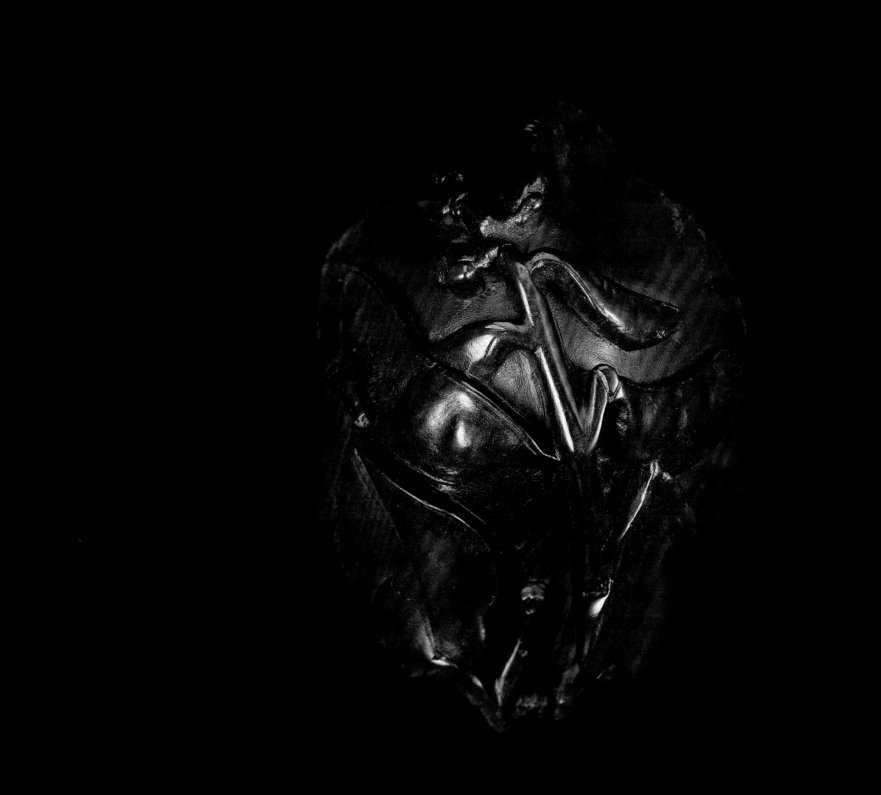

**Qing Dynasty**
*Rhino horn carving hornless dragon pattern small cup*

*L/9.5cm, H/3cm*

*The hornless dragon pattern on this rhino horn comes from patterns on ancient bronzeware. This traditional symbol is usually portrayed with an open mouth, a curled tail, and a coiled posture. It was a prevalent symbol in the Spring and Autumn and the Warring States periods, and many artworks in later periods, including rhino horn carvings, emulated the styles of the bronzes of those ancient times. Also, ancient bronzes had images of rhinos and rhino horns, indicating that ancient people were interested in rhino horns and placed importance on them.*

# 清　犀角　螭龍紋小杯

長 9.5 公分　高 3 公分

該犀角杯上的螭螭紋，原是青銅器紋飾之一。螭螭圖案表現的是傳說中的一種沒有角的龍，常作張口、蜷尾、蟠（盤）屈狀。這種紋飾盛行於春秋戰國，以二方或四方的連續排列為主，包括犀角雕刻在內的一些工藝品上的螭螭紋，仿自青銅器而作。而青銅器中也有整器作犀牛形的尊，年代較早，可知古人很早就對犀牛及犀角感興趣且非常重視。

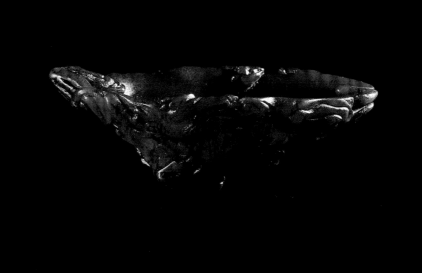

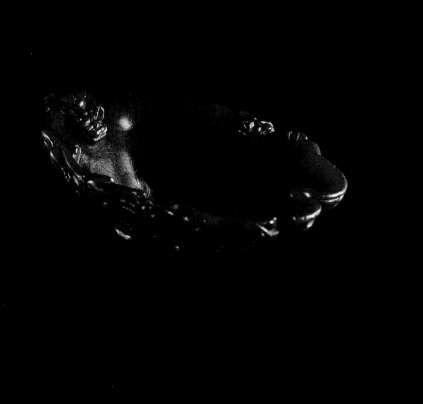

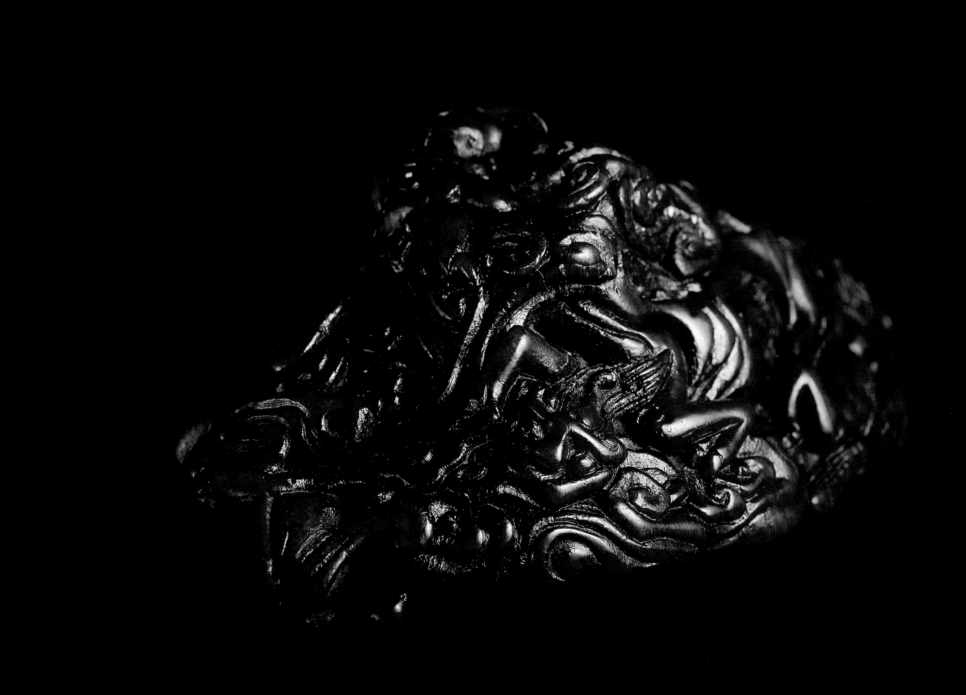

## 清　犀角　花卉小杯

長8公分　高3.2公分

此件犀角杯，整體做折枝花卉狀，犀角杯整體為花枝盤錯，杯身以浮雕、透雕手法刻畫花枝葉蔓，杯中更妙安排一橫枝。造型別緻，用刀犀利，打磨精細，雕功流暢，通過作者細膩的刻畫，梅花在枝頭綻放，杯身以浮雕、透雕方式刻出枝枒與花朵，刀法純熟樸實，整體後重而不失精巧。

### Qing Dynasty
### Rhino horn carving flowers small cup

L/8cm, H/3.2cm

This rhino horn cup is comprised entirely of floral shapes, and the cup base itself is formed of interlocking flower stems. The body of the cup is carved into flower petals using relief and openwork carving techniques, and there is a stem arranged across the middle of the cup. The shape is exquisite, the technique is detailed, the polish is refined, and the carving skill is smooth. The maker's meticulous carving creates a plum blossom blooming on its branch, and the body of the cup has the stems and flowers carved in relief and openwork styles. The workmanship is practiced and down-to-earth, and the entire piece feels substantial without sacrificing intricacy.

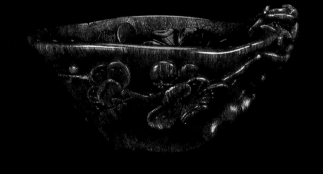

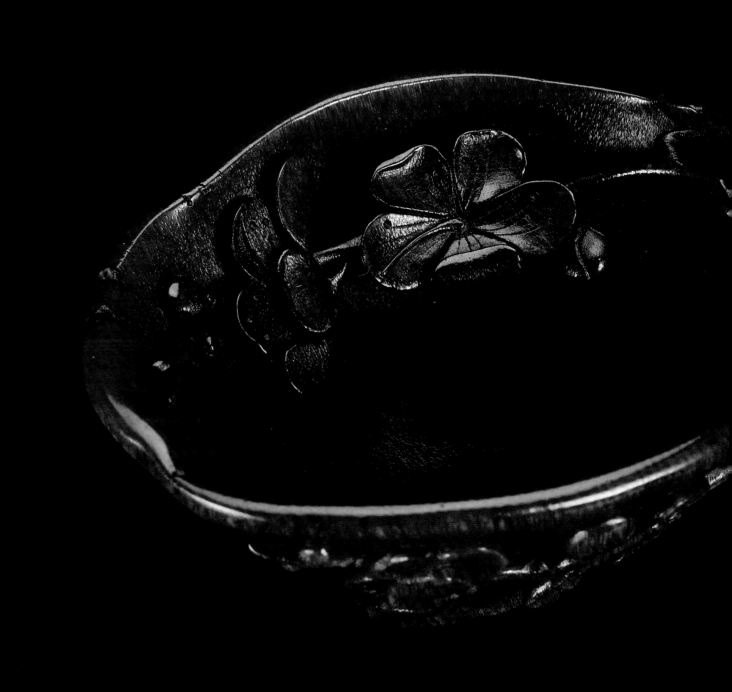

竹、木雕

竹雕，是一門古老的工藝美術。竹子的結實竿挺，虛中潔外，外表油潤，色澤近琥珀，且具有渾圓堅韌的特性，所謂「竹節心虛」，之後製成各種物件，因其典雅秀麗，更受到世人喜愛。明以前，傳世的竹刻器物和知名刻工甚少；明中葉以後至清代，竹刻名家輩出，使竹刻藝術從實用轉變成為供人們鑒賞收藏的藝術品。

明代竹刻藝術多集中在嘉定（今上海喜定縣）、金陵（今南京市）兩地，分為嘉寶派、金陵派。嘉定朱松鄰祖孫三代為深刻法（指浮雕和圓雕），金陵李耀、濮仲謙為淺刻法，加上清初張希黃的留青刻法，三者為竹刻藝術的重要表現。浮雕又分淺浮雕和高浮雕兩種，它與透雕均屬竹刻中的陽文刻法，可使器物增加立體效果。刻竹方法為鏟去較多竹地，使文飾凸起於上，並能分出層次，高浮雕可分五六層，使器物有圓渾之感，三朱竹刻用刀如運筆，生動有力，人物及動物神態自然。明代竹刻金陵派創始人濮仲謙，刻法與嘉寶派不同，不事精雕細琢，只就其天然形態，稍加鑿磨，作品略施刀刻即生自然之趣。金陵派的主要技法為淺刻，即竹刻中的陰文刻法。這種刻法不僅有線也有面，刻出的景物可再現書畫的筆情墨趣。清中期竹刻工藝出現了留青刻法，也稱貼簧、文竹、竹簧，經煮、曬、壓、膠合或鑲嵌在木胎及竹胎器物上，然後磨光，再在上面雕刻書畫紋飾，由於簧色潔淨無瑕，嫩簧嬌潤，宛如象牙。

木雕工藝是以各種木材及樹根為雕刻用材，是傳統雕刻工藝中的重要門類。木雕歷史悠久，早在河姆渡文化遺即見出土木雕魚。宋代以降，都用組織細密的木材雕刻，如黃楊木、檀香木等，後輸入內地的硬質木材，使木雕工藝得以長足發展，用料有紫檀木、烏木、紅木、雞翅木、沉香木、楠木等，最常用的則為紫檀與黃楊木。紫檀木是世界上最名貴的木材之一，主要產於南洋群島及廣西、湖南、湖北等地，屬常綠亞喬木，生長很慢，經數百年才成材。紫檀木新材色紅，老材色紫，一般呈犀牛角色，鬃眼細密、木質堅重。由於紫檀木色調深沉，紋理織細浮動、變化無窮，所製器物大多採用光素、顯得大方穩重。若雕花過多，反掩蓋木質本身紋理與色彩。紫檀木的利用在我國有悠久的歷史，但專供欣賞，以怡情悅目、陶冶心性為目的而製作的雕刻品，直到明清才形成規模，主要集中在廣州、蘇州、揚州、南京及北京等地。

國立歷史博物館研究人員

蔡耀慶

It is an evergreen arborescent tree which grows slowly, and it usually takes hundreds of years for a tree to grow to usefulness. Red sandalwood is red when it is freshly cut, and it becomes violet as it ages. It usually has a rhino horn color, with fine pores and a solid texture. Since red sandalwood has dark colors, the texture is fine and varied, so the objects made out of it are mostly shiny and feel solemn and tasteful. If the carving is too fancy, it will hide the wood's natural texture and color. The use of red sandalwood has a long history in China, but it was only used for ornamental items at first. Not until the Ming and Qing Dynasties was it used more abundantly for making artistic objects. This art was mostly concentrated in the regions of Guangzhou, Suzhou, Yangzhou, Nanjing, and Beijing.

**Tsai Yao-Ching**

**Assistant,**
**National Museum of History**

# The Art of Bamboo and Wood Carving

Bamboo carving is an ancient craft. Bamboo is straight, hollow, and smooth, and has a color like amber. It is also very solid and strong, and items made out of bamboo are well loved because of their elegance and beauty. Before the Ming Dynasty, collected bamboo carvings and famous carving artists were rare, but, from the middle of the Ming Dynasty to the Qing Dynasty, famous bamboo carving artists appeared one after the other, causing bamboo carving to be transformed from a practical art into an art of treasured and praised masterpieces.

Ming Dynasty bamboo carving was mostly concentrated in the two regions of Jiading (present day Xiding County, Shanghai) and Jinling (present day Nanjing), divided into the two schools of the Jiabao school and the Jinling school. Excellent contributions to the art of bamboo carving were made by the deep relief style (relief carving and sculpting) of Jiading's Zhu Song-Lin and his son and grandson, the shallow relief style of Jinling's Li Yao and Pu Zhong-Qian, and the liuqing style of the early Qing Dynasty's Zhang Xi-Huang. Relief carving is divided into two types: shallow relief and high relief, and, like openwork carving, it is an embossing style and can give artworks a more three-dimensional feel. The method for bamboo carving is to chip away relatively more of the bamboo surface so that the ornamentation protrudes on top. Different layers can also be created, with five or six levels in high relief carving, giving the object a natural feeling. The technique of the three Zhus involved using the knife like a paintbrush, giving the works a lively feeling with naturalistic poses for the human and animal figures. The carving technique of Pu Zhong-Qian was different from that of the Jiabao school. Pu's technique did not emphasize detailed carving, but instead valued the natural shape of the material, with only a slight amount of chiseling or grinding. The artworks need only a little carving to bring out their natural beauty, making them elegant and attractive. The main carving technique of the Jinling school was shallow relief, which is the intaglio carving method. This type of carving technique uses lines and planes, and the scenes that are carved out have the feel of calligraphy and painting. The liuqing style of bamboo carving appeared in the Qing Dynasty. After being boiled, sun-dried, and pressed, the bamboo is glued or inlaid on a piece of wood or another piece of bamboo. Then it is polished, and calligraphy-type decorations are finally carved on the top. Because the color is pure and flawless, the tender bamboo is as smooth as ivory.

The art of wood carving uses all types of woods and tree roots as its carving material. It is an important form of traditional carving. Wood carving has a long history;  evidence of carved wooden fish can be traced as far back as the Hemudu culture. After the Song Dynasty, finely structured wood, such as boxwood and sandalwood, was used for wood carving. Later, imported hardwood material allowed the art of wood carving to develop by leaps and bounds, with material such as red sandalwood, ebony, redwood, chicken wing wood, aloeswood, and camphor wood. The most commonly used were red sandalwood and boxwood. Red sandalwood is one of the world's most valuable and rare woods, and it is mainly produced in the  islands of the South Pacific and in Guangxi, Hunan, and Hubei in China.

# 明　竹雕　松下高士筆筒　顧珏款

徑6公分　高14.5公分

顧珏，字（號）宗玉，約康熙、雍正時人，繼承朱三松及沈兼技法，並加以發揚。《竹人錄》：「朱沈相承，平澹天真，純以韻勝；珏則刻露精深，細入毫髮，一器必經二載而成，是又不襲前人窠臼，而能獨立門庭者。戲仿靈璧英州石。以沉檀香黃楊木製為奇峰。真有山高月小、水落石出之致，其遺蹟槎里羅氏收蓄最富。余少時曾見，縮臨李昭道棧道圖筆斗，老樹危橋，懸崖絕澗，作數十層，轉折望之窈然而深，尤為奇絕。」顧珏活躍於康熙年間，作品以清代槎溪羅氏收藏最多，惜毀於火，所以傳世極少。

本器施以「深刻浮雕法」鐫製。深至數層，人、松、石等景略傾「半圓雕法」，配以「淺刻法」鈎澀草、樹根；整器藉之豐富技法，甚為穠華，堪為三朱之後減地鏤雕法再創高峰代表之作。

觀本器所刻人物場景，五名高士身著明代服冠，明式座椅，松下聚談，立意題材類似取自文徵明「松下高士」圖，正德十三年二月十九日，文徵明與好友蔡羽、王守、王寵、湯珍等人至無錫惠山遊覽，松下品茗飲茶，吟詩唱和，十分相得。

## Ming Dynasty
### Bamboo carving scholars under a pine tree brush holder, Gu Jue signature

*Diam./6cm, H/14.5cm*

*Gu Jue, also known as Zong Yu, lived in the times of Emperors Kangxi and Yongzheng. He continued the techniques of Zhu San-Song and Shen Jian, and improved on them. The Zhu Ren Lu describes his work as taking after Zhu and Shen, while being simple, graceful, exquisite, highly sought-after, and original. He emulated the style of Lingbi Yingzhou stone carvings. He created masterpieces from sandalwood and red sandalwood. He created very lifelike multi-layered scenes. The book also says his work was the finest example of the highest skill in bamboo carving. Gu Jue was active in the time of Emperor Kangxi, and there was one collector in the Qing Dynasty who had collected a great number of his works. Unfortunately most were lost in a fire, so they are now very rare.*

*This piece was created using the deep relief carving technique. Its depth has many levels, and the scenes of people, pine trees, and rocks are carved in an almost semi-sculpture-like carving technique, matched with grass and tree roots created with the shallow carving technique. The diverse techniques of the entire piece are very rich. It can be said to be another peak in the jiandi carving style after the time of the three Zhu's. Looking at the scene of human figures on this piece, we see that the five scholars are wearing Ming dynasty dress and caps and sitting on Ming-style chairs while talking. This theme is taken from Wen Zheng-Ming's Scholars Under a Pine Tree painting, inspired by a tour taken by that painter with four of his scholarly friends during the Ming Dynasty.*

## Qing Dynasty
## Bamboo carving light boat skimming past ten thousand sombre crags brush holder,
## Xi Huang signature

*Diam./11cm, H/15.6cm*

*The earliest example of liuqing-style embossed bamboo carving is a bamboo flute from the Tang Dynasty, housed at the Shousouin, in Japan. Very few other liuqing-style embossed bamboo carvings, however, have been found from the later Song, Yuan, Ming, and early Qing dynasties. With the appearance of the late Ming bamboo carving artist, Zhang Xi-Huang, the liuqing-style technique once again gained prominence. Zhang's name is not recorded in Ming Dynasty records, and Qing Dynasty records only record the name Zhang, without listing his background. His history and birthplace remain a mystery to this day. Chu De-Yi wrote in Zhu Ren Xu Lu (published in 1930) that Zhang Xi-Huang's history could not be determined, and reports that he was from Jiangyin could not be completely trusted. Zhang was the founder of the liuqing embossed bamboo carving style, and his compositions resemble the style of the Tang Dynasty's Li Zhao-Dao. He was most adept at using the liuqing bas-relief carving technique to carve scenes like mountains, trees and stones, landscapes and figures, and buildings and pagodas, blending carving and painting into one in the perfect example of the liuqing technique.*

*After the time of Zhang, liuqing-style bamboo carving once again lost its popularity. It did not rise in prominence again until the late-middle Qing Dynasty, when it rose to an extremely high level as one of the representative technical arts of the late Qing Dynasty. By the Jiadao era, it was very popular, and pieces by Zhang Xi-Huang became very fashionable collector's pieces. By the Republic of China era, it still had not waned, with famous liuqing-style artists like Shang Xun, Zhang Yu-Shan, Jin Shao-Tang, and Jin Shao-Fang appearing on the scene.*

*The body of this Zhang Xi-Huang liuqing bamboo carving brush holder has been slightly damaged with age. The colors are solemn and the shell is shiny and smooth. The entire piece is covered with a liuqing-style bamboo carving with a tightly ordered composition. The carving technique is exquisite, expressing the style of ancient landscape paintings in an elegant and profound scene.*

# 清 竹雕 輕舟已過萬重山筆筒 希黃款

徑11公分　高15.6公分

留青陽文，最早可見於日本正倉院藏唐代竹刻尺八。但自此之後，宋、元、明至清代前半期，均甚少發現其他留青竹刻，直至明末竹刻家張希黃出現，留青技藝得以再次發光發熱。明人筆記，未見張氏之名，清代文獻，亦只見張氏之名，而無記載張氏為何時人，其履歷、籍貫，至今成謎。褚德彝《竹人續錄》（一九三〇年出版）云：「張希黃，里貫不可攷，據粥（鬻）古人云，是江陰人，然未敢深信也」，其名亦無人知者。」張氏為留青陽文的創始者，構圖有唐代李昭道風格。他最擅長的是利用留青淺浮雕技法，刻遠山、樹石、山水人物、樓閣亭台等景物，將雕刻與繪畫融為一體，為留青技法的典範。

張氏之後，留青竹刻技術再次消退，直至清代中晚期才告復興，而且水平極高，為清代晚期工藝美術的代表之一，嘉道以後，大行其道，張氏仿作甚受藏家喜愛，至民國而不衰，其他留青竹刻名家，有尚勛、張玉山、金紹堂、金紹坊等人。

本件希黃款留青竹刻筆筒，因年代已久，筒身略有裂痕，色調穆沉，皮殼瑩潤，全器去地留青竹刻山水圖案，構圖佈局緊湊，刀法精巧細膩，傳達出古典文人山水意境，境界高雅深幽。

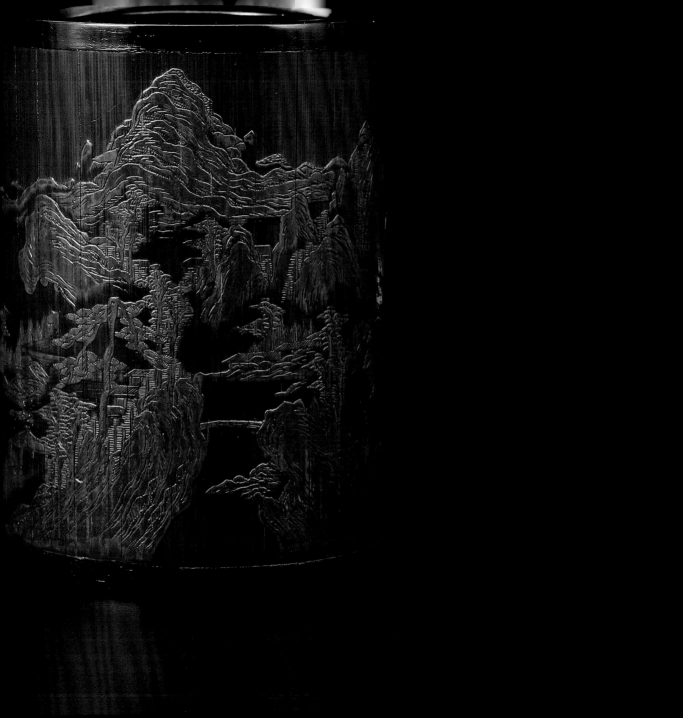

*Qing Dynasty*
*Bamboo carving Guanyin seated statue*

*W/15cm, H/20cm*

*In this Guanyin bamboo carving, one hand holds a scroll. The figure is seated in a half-lotus position on a rush cushion, with the right hand resting on the right knee and the head slanted down with a peaceful expression in which the eyes are gazing downward. The body is carved very fluidly, making this a solemn Buddhist statue.*

此座觀音竹雕，手持捲軸，以半跏趺坐姿坐於蒲團上，右手扶右膝，頭略俯，目下斂，神情沉靜。通身刻畫線條流暢，法相莊嚴。

**清 竹雕 漁翁得利 小松款**

長 10 公分　高 6.5 公分

作者運用圓雕手法，刀工犀利，線條勁挺，技藝嫻熟，造型獨特。巧妙地利用竹子的自然紋理、色澤加以表現，雕琢精湛，令人讚歎。作品的重點精在頭部，首先賦予面部表情，眉目之間透露著內在的感情。在老人與稚子的表現對比下，更加突顯工藝師的卓越。在藝術造型與裝飾上取得了動靜有致，形態若生，結構嚴謹，使作品更具有古樸的魅力。

*Qing Dynasty*
*Bamboo carving, Xiao Song signature,*
*"the fisherman profits"*

*L/10cm, H/6.5cm*

*The artist used a sculpture-like carving technique with fine carving work, bold lines, sensitive workmanship, and a unique shape. The bamboo's natural texture and color is cleverly used, with extraordinarily exquisite carving. The focus of this piece is the head, as the viewer first notices the facial expression, which reveals some inner feelings. In terms of artistic style and decorative style, this piece achieves a remarkable liveliness and a reserved structure that give it a simple charm.*

## Qing Dynasty
### Bamboo carving human figure

*W/5cm, H/5.4cm*

This is a sculpture of a son with two flowing braids, raising his head in an expression of delight. He is kneeling on a bamboo basket and it seems like there's something trying to come out of it. Both hands are placed on the basket and the expression is one of excitement. The face is very lively and the carving technique is exquisite and masterful.

清　竹雕　人物

寬5公分　高5.4公分

圓雕一子，雙辮垂髻，仰頭表情大樂，雙腳跪壓在竹籃上，似乎籃中有物急欲跳脫，復以雙手抵住竹籃，興奮之情溢於顏外。面容生動，雕刻精細傳神。

# 清　竹根　壽星

寬15公分　高17.8公分

*Qing Dynasty*
*Bamboo root God of longevity*

*W/15cm, H/17.8cm*

*The god of longevity has a protruding crown, a wide brow and large ears, long eyebrows and a wide nose, a small, slightly smiling mouth, a long beard, and kind eyes. The right hand has a walking stick and the left hand holds a longevity peach. The waist is wide and, the clothing flows freely, giving it a majestic air. There are shoes on both feet, and the base is carved into a cloud with a heavenly crane standing on the side.*

作品以竹根為材料，活用其堅實與纖絲的紋理，刻剔出壽者福慧雙臻之態。壽星頭頂頂隆突，廣額大耳，長眉寬鼻，小口微張，長髯過胸，慈眉善目。右手握一靈芝拐杖，左手執一帶葉壽桃。腰間寬厚，衣衫順勢垂落，一派雍容大度，雙腳著鞋，底座刻成雲朵，身旁有仙鶴相伴。

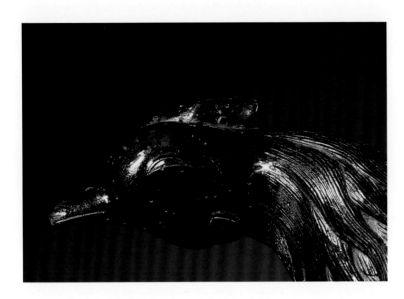

長34公分

# 清 竹雕 鳳凰獻瑞

本件竹雕雙鳳，大小雙鳳構圖，左呼右應，虛實相生；鳳鳥羽飾，精細婉約，呈現太平盛世、吉祥富貴氣息。全器品像完整，包漿玉潤，尺寸大器，為傳統竹根圓雕難得佳作。

《說文解字》中講：「鳳，神鳥也。」古人賦予它全身各部位以深刻的吉祥寓意。比如，鳳冠似靈芝表示事事稱心如意；鳳嘴可鳴叫動人的聲音，呼喚凰的到來，即所謂的「鳳求凰」，因此是美好愛情的象徵；長長的尾羽，如綬帶象徵著長壽；雙翅似大鵬展翅，表示事業發達、前程遠大；鳳身如雞身代表著吉祥。《大戴禮》曰：「羽蟲三百六十，鳳凰為長。」正所謂「百鳥朝鳳」。正于此，在百姓的眼中，鳳凰象徵著高貴、喜慶和吉祥。《說文解字》說：「見（鳳凰）則天下大安寧」。百姓將鳳凰視為預示天下太平的祥瑞之鳥。因此，在生活中，常用鳳凰作裝飾圖案。

## Qing Dynasty
## Bamboo carving phoenix presents beneficence

*L/34cm*

*This piece is a bamboo carving of a pair of phoenixes, one larger than the other, in a lifelike pose. The feathers on the phoenixes are fine and subtle, expressing the wish for peace and good fortune for the world . The whole piece seems complete and smooth with an attractive size. It is a rare work of traditional bamboo root sculpture.*

*The Shuo Wen Jie Zi says that the phoenix is a heavenly bird. Ancient artists created every part of its body to symbolize a deep sense of auspiciousness. The phoenix's crown, for example seems to convey a sense of contentment in all things. The male phoenix can make a moving cry that calls the female phoenix, so it is seen as a symbol of true love. The long tail feathers symbolize long life. The great wings indicate success in future ventures. The chicken-like body symbolizes good luck. The Da Dai Li says that the phoenix is the king of the bird world. In folk culture, the phoenix symbolizes nobility, love, and good fortune. The Shuo Wen Jie Zi says that sighting a phoenix means that there will be peace in the world. The common people saw the phoenix as an auspicious bird that portended peace. In daily life, therefore, phoenixes ,are often used in decorative patterns.*

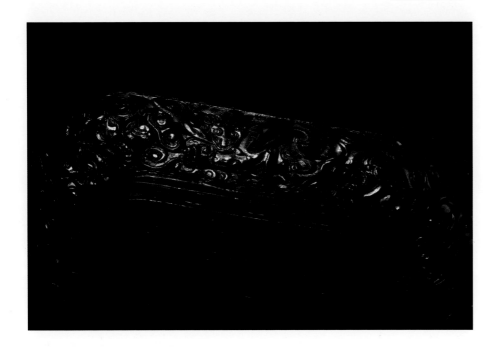

# 明 萬曆 紫檀木 香盤

長26.5公分　寬17.5公分　高3公分

香盤，是焚香用的扁平承盤，多以木料或金屬製成。此器由紫檀一木挖成，從其器寬達十八公分觀之，可知耗材甚鉅，非宮廷或王公貴族不可得。器形與雕刻內容仿明代葵瓣式雕漆盤，但雕刻採相反手法，以去地陽紋法巧雕花卉雲紋為飾，呈現另種審美意趣。明、清二朝，紫檀、黃花梨等貴重硬木多作家具或文房等器用，家具尤為耗材，凡剩餘小料、邊材等，均不忍棄之，匠意多能巧思為器，甚殊可貴。文房中雅翫中，除筆筒需一木挖鑿成器外，多上述此類之作，然而此香盤與之相比，其器度與貴重不言而喻。盤底銘刻「萬曆元年　仲秋圓吳門李中父製于竹書山房」。

## Ming Dynasty Wanli Era
## Red sandalwood incense tray

*L/26.5cm, W/17.5cm, H/3cm*

*The incense tray is a flat tray usually made of wood or metal used for burning incense. This piece was carved from a single piece of wood, and judging from the 18cm width, the original material was very large, which means it could only be the property of the imperial court or some other noble house. The entire piece is carved with Ming Dynasty style flower petals, though the embossed carving technique is used here for the flower patterns, giving it a different artistic sense from those of the Ming Dynasty. Expensive hard woods, like red sandalwood and scented rosewood were usually used to make furniture or literary studio accessories in the Ming and Qing Dynasties. Making furniture uses up a great deal of material, and there are always small pieces left over. The artisans could not bear to throw them away, so they made finely crafted artworks out of them. In terms of literary studio curios, besides useful items like brush holders that need to be carved out of wood, most items were created in the aforementioned fashion. Few, however, could compare in workmanship and loftiness with this incense tray. On the bottom, it is inscribed with text identifying it as a literati study curio made during the reign of Emperor Wanli.*

## Qing Dynasty
## Red sandalwood cloud and dragon pattern imperial seal box

*L/22cm, W/21.5cm, H/24cm*

*Traditional seal boxes are usually square-shaped with a roof-like cover because imperial seals are mostly square, and the seal handles are smaller than the seal. Seal boxes retained this shape until the late Qing Dynasty. This piece has a roof shape on the top of its cover, but the cover goes all the way to the base of the box in this case, which is a different kind of style and is a convenient design for storing and removing large seals from the box. The entire cover is exquisitely carved with the five-clawed dragon and cloud pattern, displaying the noble atmosphere of the imperial court.*

# 清 紫檀木 雲龍紋璽印盒

長22公分　寬21.5公分　高24公分

傳統印匣，多為方形盝頂式，因印璽多作方形，印鈕又總小於印身，故匣蓋多造盝頂形式樣，直至清晚期，印匣仍保留此種形式。本器雖同為盝頂，但因其罩蓋方式不同，採明高濂所謂之「罩蓋式」，亦就是匣蓋將匣底完全罩蓋於底部，此亦為印匣之另一種形式，為方便大形璽印放置與拿取之設計。全器罩蓋四面精雕五爪雲龍紋，雕工精細繁複，呈現宮廷華貴氣質。

## Qing Dynasty
### Red sandalwood cloud and dragon pattern square box

*L/21.5cm, W/19cm, H/7.5cm*

This red sandalwood cloud and dragon pattern square box has symmetrical dimensions and a substantial feel. The cover has a five-clawed dragon with a formidable presence that goes well with the red sandalwood material in which it is carved . The cloud and dragon pattern is carved with great skill. It has a refined and ordered composition, with the curling dragon body and the propitious clouds made with the finest carving technique, expressing power and glory. The box and cover fit perfectly, giving it a sense of classic nobility that goes well with its fine material.

# 清　紫檀木　雲龍紋方盒

長21.5公分　寬19公分　高7.5公分

本件紫檀雲龍文方盒，尺寸方正，用料厚實。盒蓋欑框打槽裝板，蓋面以紫檀雕刻雲龍紋，五爪蟠龍，氣度恢弘，恰與紫檀大料相輝映。所雕雲龍紋，雕作圓熟，構圖疏密有緻，蟠龍團繞婉轉，麟趾耀光，祥雲朵朵，展現俐落刀法，簇擁團龍，祥至生輝。木作樺鉚精到，接合細密，加以選料甚精，文華自顯，典雅貴氣。

清　紫檀木　「函」形套盒組

軸套：長22.2公分　寬8.4公分

函套：長16.5公分　寬11公分　高7.3公分

「函套」為古時用來裝放書籍、畫軸之裝禎器，為文人書房常見擺設實用物。函套的種類又有書套、紙匣、木匣、夾板等式樣。

本件書畫「函」形套盒組，一為書函式「方盒」，一為軸套式「套盒」。此套方盒與套盒外觀仿傚「函套」式樣唯妙唯肖，取材考究，設計精緻，增添蒐藏稀珍之感。此類設計亦見於清宮廷漆器工藝，為故宮盒型器物的形式之一，常作古玩、擺件、小件雜項收藏盒用。軸套式「套盒」其下層為雙軸並置式樣，上層則為單軸設計，盒蓋開啟採掀蓋對合方式，在使用上，上層套盒恰又為下層套盒之蓋鈕設計，極具巧思。整體外觀取硬木薄削拼接，工藝精良，觸感圓潤，配以陰雕迴紋邊飾，典雅大方。

## Qing Dynasty
### Red sandalwood  "Han-tao" curio cabinet

*Scroll case: L/22.2cm, W/8.4cm   Book case: L/16.5cm, W/11cm, H/7.3cm*

*In ancient times, the container named "Han-tao" was for the storage of books or scrolls and a practical artifact commonly found in literati's study. Types of Han-tao include book cases, paper cases, wooden cases, and clipboard cases.*

*This set of "Han"-shaped curio cabinets includes one "square box" in the shape of book case and one scroll-shaped case. The form of this curio cabinet set is a vivid imitation of "Han-tao." With its choice material and elegant craftsmanship, this set is a rare piece to be collected. Similar design of this set is also found in the Qing imperial lacquer wares and regarded as one form of box-shaped artifacts in the royal court. The lower deck of the scroll-shape case shows the shape of two scrolls, while the upper deck shows only one scroll. The upper deck also serves as the lid for the lower deck, which is a rare and smart feature for the artifact of its kind. The material is hard wood thinly pared and pieced together. The craftsmanship is exquisite and the texture is smooth. It is decorated with rectangular spirals carved in relief, making it elegant and tasteful.*

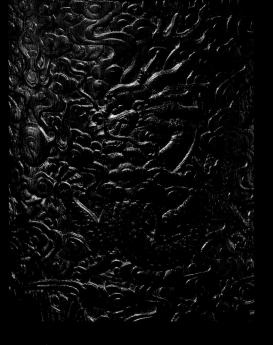

*Qing Dynasty*
*Red sandalwood seawater cloud and dragon pattern brush holder*

*H/15.5cm, Depth/14cm*

*After the Ming and Qing Dynasties, the art of making brush holders no longer strictly followed its utilitarian purpose, and it became one of the many decorations on display in the literati study. During the Qianlong era, wooden brush holders were mostly made of hard woods like red sandalwood, mahogany, rosewood, ebony, boxwood, and other materials. Red sandalwood was generally the most popular material. Bamboo carving brush holders were finely carved with floral patterns, human figures, or landscapes, and were generally the most exquisite. In addition, jade was also used as a material for brush holders, but the material sources were scarce and the workmanship had to be more refined. This red sandalwood brush holder uses the finest material, with a beautiful texture and very fine ox-hair pattern. It is uniformly carved with a seawater cloud and dragon pattern, reflecting the nobility of the palace with its majestic beauty. The carving technique is practiced and natural, with lively layers, making it a fine piece of literati study ornamentation.*

明清以降，筆筒之工藝已漸失其實用功能，而成書齋案頭陳設之一部份，漸而多以擺件之姿列於文人書房收藏陳設品列。乾隆時代木製筆筒多選硬木為材，如紫檀、紅木、花梨、烏木、黃楊及其他材質多有運用。一般以紫檀最受歡迎；竹製筆筒則以細雕花紋紋者較珍貴，或雕人物，或構山水，總能盡其雅致。另外玉製筆筒亦甚為流行，不但選料精嚴，作工也是空絕前後。本件紫檀筆筒，選料極精，紋理華美，牛毛紋綿密細緻，更勝純取大料。通體滿雕海水雲龍紋，盡顯宮廷貴氣，華美沉穆。刀法熟練自然，層次活耀，面面都可觀賞，實為書齋陳設難得佳器。

## Qing Dynasty
## Boxwood carving human figures

*H / 19cm*

*Boxwood carving is a folk handicraft that uses boxwood for its carving material. Boxwood is known as a wood that never produces large quantities of material for carving use. It is one of the famous, "three carving materials of Zhejiang," along with Dongyang wood and Qingtian stone. Boxwood material is firm and bright, with a fine texture and yellow luster, giving it an ivory-like effect that is very suitable for carving small ornaments. Its luster deepens as it ages, making it look elegantly rustic.*

*These boxwood carving pieces are delicately carved into a boy and girl holding lotus flowers and looking at each other with heads bowed. The expressions are full of youthful vigor and the postures are relaxed, showing the carving style and aesthetics of wood carving in the Ming and Qing Dynasties.*

清　黃楊木　木雕人物

高19公分

黃楊木雕是以黃楊木做雕刻材料的民間工藝品，素有「千年黃楊難做拍」（樂器中的一種拍子）的說法以及「千年矮」之別稱，與東陽木雕、青田石雕並稱「浙江三雕」。黃楊木質地堅韌並光潔，紋理細密，硬度適中，色黃溫潤，具有象牙效果，極適宜刻雕小型陳設品，特別是隨著年代的久遠，色澤愈深，古樸典雅。

本件黃楊木雕作品，精雕童女二位，分持蓮花返頸相望，面貌清秀，身姿飄逸，展現明清木雕刻共同風格及審美趣味。

During the Ming and Qing Dynasties, maritime traffic with Europe was becoming more and more frequent, and, as foreign ambassadors and missionaries made the journey to visit the imperial court, they introduced European painting techniques and production techniques. Because of the increasingly high quality of all kinds of techniques, the fondness of Qing Dynasty nobles and officials for artworks and artistic techniques began to be oriented toward fancier and more refined tastes. The preferences of the imperial family made expensive materials like jade, ivory, wood, and silk more rare and precious because, on one hand, the tastes of artists and nobles combined into the creation of lofty and beautiful ornamental effects, and the folk aesthetics of the common people were also influenced. Artists used clever techniques to produce works of marvelous craftsmanship. While this conformed with the preferences of the nobles, it also allowed wealthy merchants, prominent families, and upper class officials and intellectuals to try to outdo each other in their pursuit of art appreciation within mainstream aesthetics.

The contents of ancient paintings were informed by the will of the rulers. If the lofty emperor hoped to accomplish some political achievement or to be seen as an upright ruler, then he would adopt the political method reflected in classical Confucian thought, that says, "Whatever people desire is always in my heart," and cause paintings to perform the extremely important duty of the propagation of decrees or the edification of the public. The figures, histories, or events depicted by painters became the tool for, "promoting moral relations and enlightenment". Imperial court painters were also responsible for the task of recording in painting form the accomplishments and important events in the lives of the emperor and the nobles. Imperial craftsmen usually manifested the ambitions of the nobles in paintings, silk tapestries, red lacquer, and carvings in all kinds of precious materials. The subjects of these paintings were auspicious celebration and perfect happiness, which is consistent with the beautiful wishes for life found in civilian art, though the contrasted sharply with the plain styles of civilian art.

In general, although the upper classes of the Ming and Qing Dynasties still held the traditional values of their predecessors in terms of the concept of collecting and appreciating beautiful artworks, the influence of the production techniques and concepts of the West injected new elements in the artistic styles and techniques of these periods that produced more diverse ideas on the foundation of the traditions of previous dynasties.

# 清 雍正 清世宗朝服立像

高215公分 寬115公分　紙本設色

清世宗雍正皇帝胤禛，是滿清入關後第三代皇帝，康熙四子，生於康熙十七年（一六七八年）十月三十日，自幼習經書、曉忠孝大義，在位十三年（一七二二——一七三五年），理政不怠，並將耶穌會傳教士趕回澳門。雍正曾禁教，下令關閉教堂，並創「儲位密建」及「密褶」制，為「康乾盛世」開承先啟後之功。

此幀立像為雍正身著明黃色冬朝袍的寫生，頭戴大朝大祭用的薰貂通天朝冠，冠檐上折，純金冠頂滿鑲東珠，頸掛朝日用珊瑚朝珠，並著紫貂滾邊朝日紅色披領，腰繫明黃色吉服帶，其上有鏤金版四，正中為鑲東珠十字形圓版，鏤金帶版上則繫有遊牧文化遺存象徵的佩文綉，燧觽萬削。雍正這身吉服打扮是為喜慶日子所穿著。圖像內容和乾隆登基時郎世寧所繪「乾隆朝服像」完全一致。

這幀世宗朝服立像的繪畫表現形式，和習見雍正朝善繪的御史莽鵠立所作，中式平塗繪畫表現手法截然不同，從面容明暗的陰影表現及衣褶立體感觀之，是採用西洋遠近透視手段繪製。北京故宮所藏郎世寧於乾隆二十五歲登基時所繪「乾隆朝服像」與本幀立像，除開一坐立及臉像不同外，其他乃至手執朝珠的位置及衣袖縐褶反光的細節，都如出一轍。這類郎世寧歐西風格的帝王肖像畫，除上述之例外，北京故宮的「清高宗孝賢純皇后朝服像」及現藏美國克利夫蘭美術館、郎世寧繪於乾隆元年（一七三六年）八月吉日的乾隆、孝賢純皇后及十一嬪妃半身像的手卷「心寫治平圖」，都是最佳的寫照。

郎世寧于康熙五十四年（一七一五年）來華傳教，被召入內廷為畫院供奉，歷經康、雍、乾三朝，乾隆三十一年（一七六六年）卒於北京。同一時期的內廷恭奉王致誠（Jean-Denis Attiret，一七○二——一七六八年）在一七四三年致達素（d'Assaut）信函中曾提及「在我到此之前的夏天，繪製了皇帝及皇妃的肖像，作者是我會（耶穌會）修士，來自義大利非常出色的畫師郎世寧。我現在和他在一起……。」

這幀「清世宗朝服立像」不同於常見的皇帝坐像，而是採用西方立像形式，並且將地毯的花紋圖案裝飾於畫像的邊框，做為替代中式裱框的綾布紋樣，確實是超乎尋常，是郎世寧為乾隆登基所繪製一系列寫生肖像，及先帝御容的海外遺珍。

*Qing Dynasty Yongzheng Era*
*"Standing Portrait of Emperor Yongzheng in Court Robes"*
*Ink and color on paper*

*H/215cm, W/115cm*

*Emperor Yongzheng was the third generation of the Manchurian emperors of the Qing Dynasty. He was born on October 30, 1678, the fourth son of Emperor Kangxi. He enjoyed studying from a young age, and he understood philosophy. During his reign (1712 – 1735), he took an active interest in governance, and he created a system for succession to the throne. Yongzheng closed Christian churches and banned missionaries.*

*This realistic portrait shows Yongzheng wearing yellow winter court robes and a black marten fur crown used for high ceremonies. The brim of the crown is folded upward, and the point of pure gold is embedded with pearls. There is a coral bead necklace around his neck, and he is draped with a red cape edged in violet marten fur. There is a yellow belt at his waist which has engraved gold with a round piece in the center inlayed with peals in the form of a cross. There is also a small bag on the carved gold belt that is symbolic of his nomadic heritage. Yongzheng is dressed in these clothes because it is a celebration. All the details of the painting are the same as the painting of Emperor Qianlong on the occasion of his ascension to the throne.*

*This portrait was painted by the imperial minister Mang Hu-Li, who was often present in Yongzheng's court, and its style is markedly different from the Chinese flat painting style. From the shades of light and shadow in the face and the 3D look of the clothing's folds, the Western painting technique of perspective can be perceived. This painting is almost identical with Guiseppe Castiglione's painting of Qianlong taking the throne at age 25 that is collected in the Beijing Palace Museum, with the only exceptions being that one is seated and the other is standing and in the facial expressions. Besides the aforementioned painting, the best examples of Guiseppe Castiglione's Western-influenced paintings are found in the portrait of Empress Xiao Xian Chun in the Beijing Palace Museum and the paintings of Qianlong, Empress Xiao Xian Chun, and court maidens found in the Cleveland Museum of Art in the USA. Guiseppe Castiglione came to China in 1715 as a missionary, and was appointed as a painter in the imperial court, where he served under emperors Kangzi, Yongzheng, and Qianlong. He died in 1766 in Beijing. A member of the imperial court at the same time, Jean-Denis Attiret, wrote a letter to d'Assaut in 1743 that described how a fellow Jesuit named Guiseppe Castiglione was the imperial portrait painter.*

*This "Standing Portrait of Emperor Yongzheng in Court Robes" is different from commonly seen imperial portraits in that it uses a Western painting style, and it uses a rug-style pattern around the edges of the painting, taking the place of Chinese style frame. It is an extraordinary painting, perhaps even more so than Guiseppe Castiglione's realistic portrait of Qianlong taking the throne and the imperial portraits found in overseas collections.*

## Yuan Dynasty
## *Yuan embroidery painting of the four joys of early spring*

*H/186cm, W/86cm*

*The theme of this embroidery painting is blooming flowers like peonies, plum blossoms, orchids, and chrysanthemums announcing the joyous news of the arrival of spring. The overall composition of flowers, stones and hills is magnificent, filling the painting while leaving blank spaces at the same time, and being both solemn and graceful. Also, there is a sense of expansion in all four directions, filling it with vigorous vitality. The technique mainly uses straight stitches, including slanting stitch, plain stitch, block shading stitch, bind off stitch, and joint stitch. The color scheme has different intricate layers of light and dark, making it serene and elegant as well as fascinating. It has imperial collection seals from Yongzheng, and even more from Qianlong.*

此件繡畫的主題是：牡丹、梅、蘭、菊等綻放丰采，報告春將來到大地的喜訊。花和石和土丘的整體構圖極其卓絕，既飽滿又疏放；既沉穩又飄逸，並且上下四方皆顯露綿延伸展之欲向，充滿蓬勃生機。技法主要採用直針系列，含纏針、平針、搶針、套針、接針等，色調則淺深有別、講究層次，幽然韻致，足耐尋味。皇帝的收藏大印從雍正的「皇四子和碩雍親王」傳到「光緒御覽之寶」，當然，乾隆占最多，如：「乾隆御覽之寶」、「古稀天子之寶」、「八徵耄念之寶」、「五福五代堂寶」等。

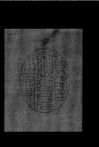

元
綉
先
春
圖
喜
四
春
圖
于
戡
甲
趙

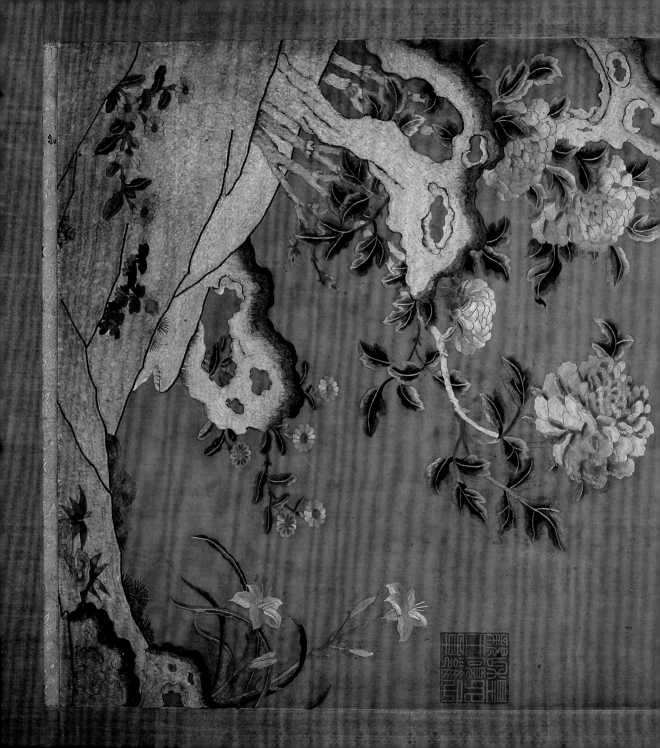

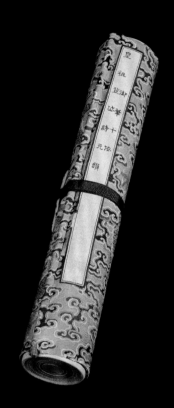

## Qing Dynasty Qianlong Era
## "Ascending Mount Tai" scroll with imperial poetry

*This Painting: L/548cm, H/36cm, Front spacer: L/90cm*

Mount Tai is a sacred peak in Shandong Province that has been the subject of veneration by emperors and the glowing descriptions of poets since the most ancient dynasties. Since it is the easternmost of the five sacred peaks, and east is the direction of the rising sun, symbolizing the birth of creation, ancient people considered Mount Tai to be the most venerable peak, the beautiful and mysterious home of the efficacious gods.

This scroll contains the words of Emperor Qianlong, and it records the poem written by the emperor upon his climb of Mount Tai. Qianlong climbed Mount Tai many times to pray for good fortune for the kingdom, and wrote many poems about it from 1748 to 1780, which shows how much the pilgrimage to Mount Tai moved him. The emperor's calligraphy style follows that of Zhao Mengfu, with slightly elongated script, and with a regular script that contains signs of running script. The running script is also mixed with a cursive script feel, with round and even stippling and subtle and smooth composition. This scroll's large characters are full and its small characters are rounded, making it a work of supreme tastefulness

泰山，《虞典》稱之為「岱宗」，《禹貢》稱為「岱」，《周禮》稱「岱山」，《詩經‧魯頌》言：「泰山岩岩，魯邦所瞻。」《爾雅》曰：「泰者，太也，謂天地太和之氣發舒。」《說苑》曰：「山者，宣也，言宣氣生萬物也。」泰山被稱為東嶽，《岱史‧形勝考》引《詩》注云：「嶽言山之尊也。東方主天地生氣，以方位別五嶽，是為天之東柱。」古人認為，東方是太陽升起的地方，是陰陽交代萬物發生之地。於是，位於東方的泰山，便成了萬物交替的群嶽之長，成了吉祥之山、神靈之宅、紫氣之源。

此長卷為乾隆所書，內容紀錄登岱山時，所作詩句。乾隆屢登泰山為國祈福，最早一首〈丹梯紆陟〉寫於一七四八年，最末一首〈六十一年〉寫於一七八〇年，內容文字全載於乾隆詩文全集。乾隆有款云：「右登岱依韻詩自戊辰至今歲，十疊已全。因彙錄成卷，弇行館以誌歲月。嗣後或復巡再過此處，重款壹天，當更拈別韻成句不繼庸，並識於此。乾隆庚子白鶴泉御筆」。長卷前題「崇情仰止」四字。乾隆書法從趙孟頫入手，字體稍長，楷書中多有行書的筆意，行書中又往往夾雜著草書的韻味，點畫圓潤均勻，結體婉轉流暢，此長卷大字飽滿，小字圓潤，成為穩貼之作。

崇情仰止

恭依

皇祖登岱詩韻 戊辰

丹梯行陟穿雲腳翠巘平臨待日頭地迥頓教塵慮淨職空惟覺色身浮果於萬古宗天下詎獨千秋鎮兗州大壯畢生景仰志可無誓句串巖留

天齊繞讓天居上進步竿尋百尺頭衆皺峯如能變化太空雲與作沉浮豈緣乘興三千仞敬識憑高十二州縱迷何能豐敢不乾坤亭裏久延留乾坤亭在岱頂以奉皇祖御書普照乾坤四大字處也

過泰山再依

皇祖詩韻 辛未

繞看積雪清峯脊又覺輕雲翳日頭豈是山靈邀客住故教嵐氣作烟浮賡吟尚愜堯登頂結攬遐思禹畫州阿那一天門〻左側雲巢三日我曾留雲巢岱頂行宮名

灰路盤旋出谷口岱宗俯視衆峯頭試回前度旋如

五福五代堂古稀天子寶

八徵耄念之寶

太上皇帝之寶

皇祖詩韻　丁丑

過泰山三依

聖蹤承古芳崇嚴
東來紫氣馬前浮
見峯頭南指遙程春曉黃
方山一帶停清蹕泰岱
懺澤于今左列州縱是瞳
季嬉莫及
觀揚敬不念深甸
靈嚴石路盤山趾齋甸西嶺
光動陌頭案術逵涇西嶺
度崒嵸不礙曉烟浮辭辛
寸意馳仙閘與地孤標俯
魯州憂樂向東來何霜著思
量結習豈徒聞

皇祖詩韻　丁丑

登泰山四依　丁丑

春月南巡限程迢題詩興
寄碧嶙頭設如雨度皆空
過今丁丑終覺一心太素浮調
聖繞辭曲阜縣登山還至
泰安州乾坤晉熙
奎章萬古留
天襟廓景仰
瞬息十春巖電影年來憂
樂憶淡頭誰能石上三生想
且看烟中九點浮幻吳仙郎
謝蓬海悩哉民瘼指徐州雲
齋州笑云此地山川景只
合驅車不合留

登泰山六依<br>
皇祖詩韻 壬午

春迹南國孤行躊搓高<br>
山仰馬頭可匹何曾吳嶺<br>
見阮成乃瀿大江浮便教<br>
一問峯号谷束許多勞里<br>
與州涛曉載登午言降那<br>
因膝霻愆眺留<br>
五嶽之中宗首出誰能昆<br>
脂興皆頭神傳杜句真績<br>
輻家擬韓文信示浮結揽<br>
聖情昭泰麓照民隱遍<br>
方州絕繩令日伊余責敢<br>
不聰瓱一意留

實此山溪瀿空庭不恩留<br>
遍泰山五依<br>
皇祖詩韻 壬午

靈巖謂是高無比更有離<br>
峯左上頭瞰魯象曾詩裏<br>
趨青齋色急跳前浮禪封<br>
玉帛奏號漢襟常耕素郡<br>
濩州保泰惟斯躬丽勉況<br>
榮昔彼志毋留<br>
兩度天門親拾級<br>
叢碑撐讀至雲頭戊辰年<br>
車郡堪道丁丑春巡以<br>
浮不改盱宵勤磨改惟期<br>
樂利永東州省方總<br>
武一心切証是無端七字<br>
留

海岱源頭已喬山嶽之雲霞
俯束灯青之齋魯浮山嶺別
陰陽分作郡星明角亢眠
為州隸今七慶廣

聖蹟留
元韻為有峯巔

大山嶺隆崇自參漢眾峯拱
揮斥駢頭春朝又覩神霄
直頭佳氣気束馬首浮愷普
東州千秋啟問登臨者幾
豫遊臻上界至今樂利溥

皇祖詩韻辛卯
登泰山八俵

豫遊本擬當銓跡 乙酉南巡回鑾
皇太后

聖壽日增曾諭余時扶
華葦遠昨春孝臣
觀因新莘泰山祠廟藏工適逢
慈闈八旬大慶泰詩門歡説
絺絺返俱由水程登陸不過數日仍可
玄暮頤誠謁至再
頤安諭欲報低廟雯竟致辭
忻介可請因頤為轉事
東輪奠新歌重叩
虞敦躬迷豈是動輕浮頤
頭

言

志養六惟體

遞箕如高嶽詎曰登封俯
遠州萬級天門攀不易行
安留地方支於低蕉添葺行館先期
吳供總息每俊府李永石耗
及供頓鋪張殺耗勤力
宮清潔呈

巖象崇崇息對面
奎文朗人臣當頭
坤四齋煙人九點選眉括匹練

三吳近署浮錢鏐

八旬開寶耀靈芳古真

神州再束此後知何 日欲
玄珠期步為 聲去 留

皇祖詩韻 丙申
登泰山九依

空後言是否殖其浮惟知
覺徽白頭上瑞古今真此
八旬五母仍康步六十六

養
志以天下況是祝
鼇殿九州代岳廟己晚申
懿惆高峯
間五藏頭入目景妄非績
欲防額停留

元黄以剃芋古時伯仰之
畫盪胸雲有君沈浮
天章詎止垂永世
遇泰山十依
聖意昭燃照下州役以九
虞喻九仍十全有待再吟留

皇祖詩韻 庚子
六十一年君道煥
高如泰岱執齋頭
仁心仁政恒垂永
今存七字
鴻麻芋古被諸州子禁印境
實行 聲去 實言務玄浮峻極玉
增鑽仰澄實末由愧遲聲去留
十全今果酬前韻 丙申

鑾誠朱久拖成

永別幻如浮徒因民顧述

吳郡便以途遶過巖州四

字廣束各已世再經不挹

重聲詞留

右登代依韻詩自戊辰至今

歲十疊已全因彙錄成卷壽

行館以誌歲月嗣後或復

巡再過此宸重勉壺天當

更拈別韻成句示後廣号

後於此

乾隆庚子白韻象御筆

沉香亭子暗如煙

黃水墨天識

如烟濃艷晴

得黑牛顏色

好胭脂不值

半文錢

唐寅折枝

牡丹小品

臣張若靄

敬摹本丹

題

本幅，紙本。縱八寸二分。橫一尺五寸二分。墨書折枝牡丹。自題「沉香亭子暗如煙。濃艷晴黃水墨天。識得

黑牛顏色好。胭脂不值半文錢。唐寅折枝牡丹小品。臣張若靄敬摹撫本。」并題。鈐印三。臣靄。餘事。小三昧。

高宗純皇帝御題「艷芳別致」，鈐寶一。乾隆宸翰。鑑藏寶璽，五全璽，寶笈三編。

張若靄（一七一三——一七四六年）字晴嵐（《讀畫輯略》作字景采，號晴嵐），安徽桐城人。相國廷玉子。

雍正十一年（一七三八年）傳臚，官禮部尚書，襲伯爵。謚文僖。以書、畫供奉內廷，一日太后出方寸之玉珮，

命書《心經》一篇。競日而就，因賜上方珍玩無算。善畫山水、花鳥，得王穀祥、周之冕遺意。卒年三十四（按

《清代畫史》、《清畫家詩史》均作三十二歲，《中國畫家人名大辭典》作三十六歲）。

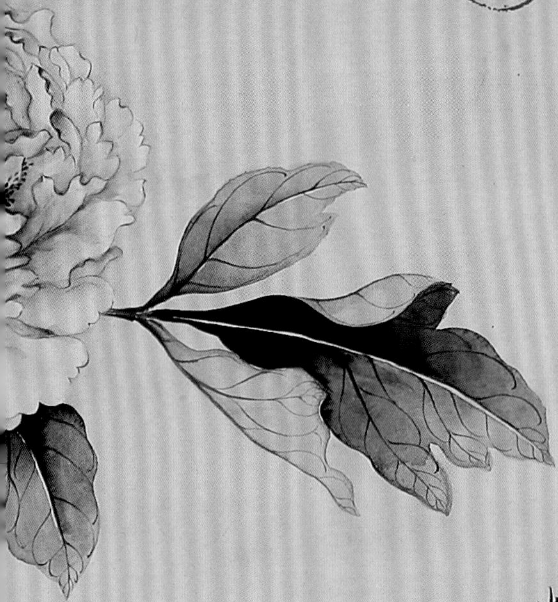

沉香亭子晴
如烟濃艷晴
薰水墨天識
得黑牛顏色
好胭脂不值
半文錢

唐寅折枝
牡丹小品
臣張若靄
敬橅本并
題

## Qing Dynasty
## Red lacquer "Returning from battle in triumph" rounded plaque

*W/99cm, H/61cm*

*This is a very intricate red lacquer wooden wall plaque. Its composition is divided into two triangular pieces on the top left and bottom right. There are curling clouds in the sky in the upper left, and the larger lower left area has a mountain range, lush trees and a scenic pavilion as the background, contrasting with the soldiers in various postures swirling around in the center. They hold bows and crossbows, as the two sides confront each other in a fierce battle. Although the technique only uses shallow relief and deep relief, its style is especially intricate. Its form is complete from every perspective. There is another plaque affixed on the top left of the center battle scene in which a verse is written in black lacquer describing the military exploits of recovering lost territory in Jinchuan. The frame of this main plaque is also made of red lacquer, and besides cloud patterns, it is also decorated with dragon, red sun, and dragon-pearl patterns. The back of the plaque is covered with black lacquer, with the eight treasures pattern of bats, fish, and treasure vase patterns painted in gold on the top, making it even more ornamental and impressive.*

這是非常講究的一件木胎剔紅橫掛屏。它先以對角構圖分出左上及右下兩個三角塊。左上的天空飄著朵朵卷雲，更大片的右下方則以層巒疊嶂、蓊鬱樹木及瞭望塔台等三者為背景，烘托著以各種搏鬥之姿繞轉於其間的兵勇戰士，他們張弓射弩、對壘交峰、戰況火熾。技法雖僅浮雕、淺雕、深雕等，然形制又是另一講究。即：表裏內外，照顧周全。在中心主題的戰役圖屏左上方貼覆另一橫板，上以黑漆寫成詩一首，跋為：「將軍阿桂奏報官軍收復小金川全境詩以誌事」。而此主圖屏外加同是剔紅的框，除卷雲紋之外尚有龍、紅日、龍珠紋等。圖屏背面木胎塗了黑漆，上有描金的蝙蝠及盤長、雙魚、寶瓶等八寶紋樣，顯示富麗輝煌氣象。

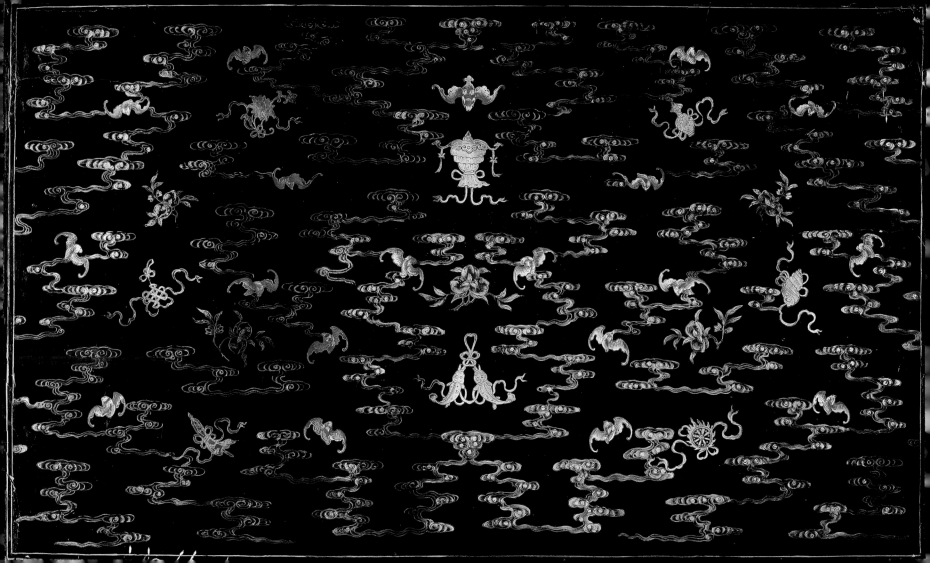

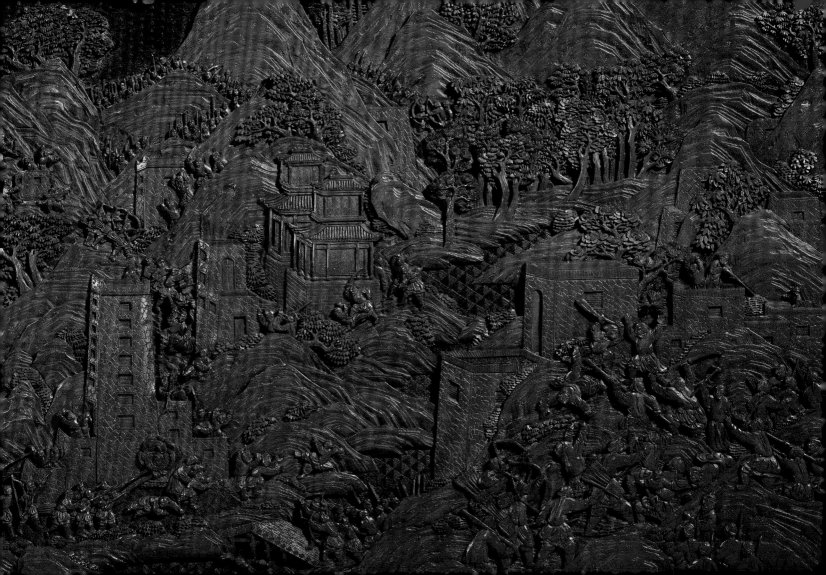

**Ming Dyansty**
**Temple wall painting**
**Fragment of Female Celestial Presenting Treasure**

*H/96cm, W/59cm    Mineral pigments*

*This wall painting was originally painted on the inside wall of a temple. It is part of a religious icon or a mural. It is one of the female celestials presenting treasure. The figure holds a tray with three tripod censers with erect handles, retaining a Yuan Dynasty style.*

*The face of the female celestial is full and round, with long eyelashes, cherry lips, and a laurel on her head. Her clothing is noble and decorative, and she has a pious expression and a delicate and graceful posture.*

*This wall painting's main colors are blue and green, and its overall atmosphere is full of simplicity. Although it is a fragment, it shows enough to display the solemn style of the Ming Dynasty religious wall paintings such as those found in Beijing's Fahai Temple and Shijiazhuang's Pilu temple.*

# 明　奉寶玉女　寺觀壁畫

高96公分　寬59公分　礦物顏料

此壁畫原應繪於寺廟道觀內壁，為宗教造像或故事中之一部，為奉寶玉女之一。手執托盤，上置三足鬲式燻爐，爐耳高聳，具元代造形遺風。

玉女面形豐滿圓潤；柳眉鳳眼、櫻桃朱唇，頭戴花冠造形飾物，服裝富貴華麗，表情虔誠，體態嫻雅典緻。

本壁畫以青綠設色為主，整體氛圍古樸凝重，雖僅為殘片，足以呈現宗教壁畫之蕭穆風格，與北京西郊法海寺及石家莊毘盧寺明代壁畫風格神似。

# 明　永樂　鎏金　銅佛

為藏密廿一度母造像之一。度母法像莊嚴，豐容厚頤，垂目微笑，頭戴寶冠，自在坐於蓮花座上。度母身佩瓔珞，右手執寶瓶，左手於胸前執手印，以鎏金製作，工藝渾厚有度，為銅佛中之精品。蓮花座面前端刻有「大明永樂年施」款，屬明代早期鎏金銅佛工藝風格。

## Ming Dynasty Yongle Era
## Gilt bronze Avalokitesvara

*H/22cm*

*This is one of the 21 forms of Tara in Tibetan Buddhism. This Tara statue is dignified, round and smooth, and substantial. The eyes are cast downward, the mouth shows a slight smile, and the head wears a crown. The figure is comfortably sitting on a lotus throne. Tara is wearing a necklace, and holds a vase in the right hand, while the left hand makes a hand gesture in front of the chest. It is made of gilt bronze, and the craftsmanship is substantial and tasteful, making it a fine piece among bronze Buddhist statues. The lotus throne has an inscription which marks it as being made in the reign of Ming Dynasty Emperor Yongle, showing it to be part of the style of gilt bronze statues of the early Ming.*

高 26 公分

明　鎏金　四臂文殊菩薩

為藏密文殊師利菩薩鎏金造像。菩薩法像莊嚴，頭戴寶冠，垂目微笑，結跏端坐於蓮花座上。文殊師利菩薩生有四臂，一手執劍，惜劍身已失，一手執蓮花，雙手於胸前執手印，以鎏金製作，工藝精巧有度，為銅佛中之精品。

**Ming Dynasty**
**Gilt bronze four-armed Manjusri Bodhisattva**

*H/26cm*

*This is a gilt bronze statue of Manjusri Bodhisattva of Tibetan Buddhism. The bodhisattva statue is dignified, with the head wearing a crown and the eyes cast downward with a slight smile. It sits in a lotus position on a lotus throne. Manjusri Bodhisattva has four arms that hold a sword, though the sword itself is unfortunately lost, and a lotus flower, while the other two hands are making gestures in front of the chest. It is made of gilt bronze using exquisite workmanship, making it a fine piece among bronze Buddhist statues.*

## Ming Dynasty
### Bronze Zhou sacrificial animal with gold and silver inlay

*W / 35cm, H / 24cm*

*This bronze sacrificial animal with gold and silver inlay is an exquisite copy by Ming Dynasty artisans of a War [States] Period sacrificial animal wine vessel with gold and silver inlay. During the Song and Ming Dynasties, [upper] classes loved ancient art, so there were many copies made of ancient bronze artifacts. Most of them were [use] in the literary studio or for decorative purposes. The style of the age they were made in is also evident [craftsmanship] of these many fine reinterpretations of ancient artifacts.*

## Qing Dynasty
### *Gilt bronze double phoenix censer stand*

*W/16.5cm, H/19cm*

*This gilt bronze censer stand was used for burning incense. The overall shape is an almost round shape on a low base. A pair of phoenixes forms the main ornamentation. Its special feature is the fine craftsmanship of the embedded decorations on the top part of the censer stand, with semiprecious stones such as coral, jasper, beeswax, lapis lazuli, white jade, and rose quartz that give it an extremely gorgeous multicolored decoration. This is the "bai bao qian" (inlay of one hundred gems) method famous in the Qing Dynasty. The creation of this work involved meticulous and time-consuming work. It would have been a utensil for a noble house.*

# 清　鎏金　雙鳳香座

寬16.5公分　高19公分

銅鎏金香座，為薰香用具。整體造型以近圓形的底座上，一雙鳳鳥構成主要紋飾，其特色是在香薰座上以精工嵌飾各種各色半寶石，有珊瑚、碧玉、蜜蠟、青金石、白玉、粉晶等，裝飾得五彩斑爛，十分華麗，此種製法是清代著名的「百寶嵌」，其製作工序上十分繁複費工，屬於豪門貴族家中的用器。

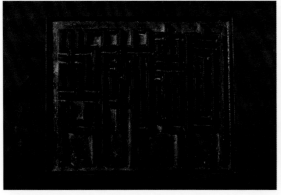 

## 清　銅灑金　三足爐

寬36.5公分　高23.5公分

銅製香爐，傳世宣德爐款式，式樣敦樸厚重，雙環耳，下配三短足，爐下設同質材之短鼓形台座。三足爐之特色在於皮色以銅灑金技法製作，色澤沉厚，光華內斂。

*Qing Dynasty*
*Bronze gold-splashed tripod burner*

*W/36.5cm, H/23.5cm*

*This is a bronze burner in the traditional Xuan De style. Its style is straightforward ands simple, with two ringed handles and three short legs below. The tripod sits on a short drum-shaped platform made of the same material. The special feature of the tripod burner is its skin color is made with the gold-splashed bronze technique, giving it a sedate luster and a reserved brilliance.*

## Qing Dynasty Qianlong Era
## "Liao" glass teat-shaped foot tripod censer, inscribed as made during the reign of Qianlong

*W/11.5cm, H/7.6cm*

*The material is called "liao", which is actually glass. In the past, all "liao" glass artworks were white. In the time of Qianlong, glassware workmanship was refined and splendid. Lead, potassium, or sodium were usually used as fluxing agents to create all kinds of glassware that was "white as suet jade, red as fire stone, green as blue jade, or yellow as chicken fat stone". Shandong's Boshan glassware used saltpetre for calcination, giving them a colorful appearance that was splendid and eye-catching. The high value placed on glassware ornaments in the early Qing Dynasty can be seen in the fact that glassware was seen as something to collect, display, appreciate, and retain value, and it was considered more valuable than porcelain. This censer with three stubby feet has handles pointed upward, signifying respect for heaven. Its legs are shaped like teats, so it is called a "teat censer". The shape is modeled after ancient bronze tripod cauldrons. This pure and elegant glassware resembles suet jade, making it a fine piece of artwork.*

清 乾隆 料 三乳足鑪 乾隆年製款

寬11.5公分 高7.6公分

料者，今之玻璃製器也。凡玻璃製器，以前皆日料器，即現在仍多以料稱也。乾隆時期料器工藝，精研秘法，魅力無限，常可用鉛、鉀、鈉等熔劑，製出「白如脂玉、紅如火齊、綠如翠玉、黃如雞油」的各色料器。山東博山的料器更用硝酸鉀鍛燒，五彩紛陳，絢麗奪目。故清初的料器精品均為藏家看中，視作珍藏、陳列、賞玩與保值的對象，甚有料作精品比清初官窯瓷器更珍罕稀貴者，可見料作精品於清初工藝品類之分量。本器三乳足鑪，朝天耳式，意寓崇敬上天，其足突出如乳頭狀，又稱乳爐，其形取自青銅鬲鼎。全器素淨，器型優雅，精作料仿脂玉，潔潤透白，品高靜肅，堪為佳作。

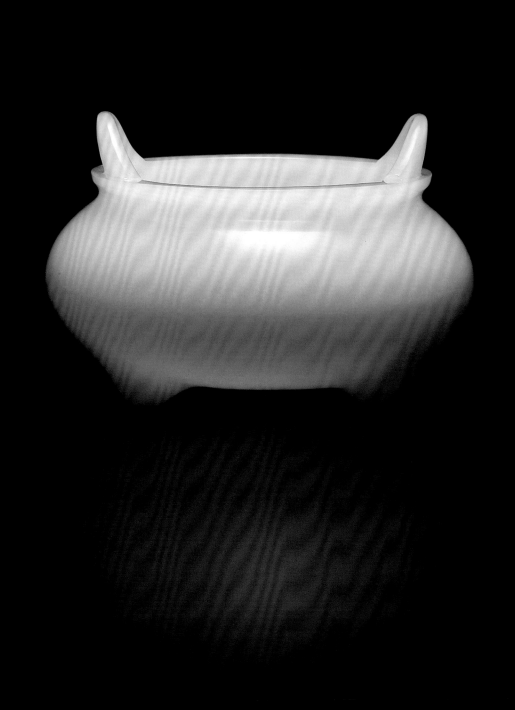

## Qing Dynasty
## Imperial Qianlong crystal medicine bottle

*W/4.1cm, H/6.5cm*

In the Qing Dynasty, sniffing snuff was a popular pastime from the emperor down to the common people, and snuff bottles made from The workmanship on this crystal bottle is exquisite. The stopper has the imperial character "yu" and the body of the bottle is inscribed with four characters meaning "septuagenarian emperor," carved in seal script. The top of the stopper has two hornless dragons which seem lively due to the material. When removing the stopper, its amethyst interior can be seen, which harmoniously fits with the overall style. The carving work for the whole piece is sophisticated, making it an excellent work of art. Because the stopper does not have a small spoon, and the bottle design makes it convenient to carry as an accessory, this bottle was probably used as a medicine bottle. The dining habits of the Qing Dynasty court were diverse, very decadent, and removed from common life, causing their health to often fail at a young age. Perhaps this was used to hold longevity pills that could be taken at any time to improve health.

# 清　水晶　御用古稀天子藥壺

寬4.1公分　高6.5公分

此壺作工精巧，通體以水晶精雕成形，壺蓋刻「御」字，壺身則有「古稀天子」四字，篆書工整，宛若其印璽再現。蓋頂刻有雙螭環立，因其材質特色而有靈動之感。解開上蓋，可見以紫水晶所製壺之內蓋，搭配合宜適度，整體刻製細膩，確實為傑出工藝之作。此壺因蓋並未有小匙的安置，而且此瓶設計方便隨身佩帶可能是作為藥壺之用。清代宮廷生活飲食豐富，而四體不勤，心血管系統、運動系統難免會過早衰退，或許正製有長壽丹丸，隨時服用以保證健康。

# 清 乾隆 瓷 珊瑚紅釉描金鼻煙壺帶剔紅盒

乾隆年製款

壺：寬4.5公分 高6公分　盒：寬11.2公分 高4.8公分

壺身為白瓷釉上彩，作太平有象，象諧「祥」之音，因此傳統習俗中象代表了吉祥。在裝飾上與象組成的圖案很多，如「太平有象」圖，是象背上駄一寶瓶。寶瓶裡的聖水，能給人間帶來祥瑞，象徵天下太平。

此鼻煙壺細緻精工，壺底有乾隆年製四字款，配上剔紅漆盒，高貴而雅緻。漆盒面精雕「寶相花」樣，層次分明，刀法細緻，繁中不紊而更顯富麗、珍貴。

## Qing Dynasty Qianlong Era
### Coral red glaze painted gold snuff bottle wit red lacquer box, inscribed as made during the reign of Qianlong

*Bottle: W/4.5cm, H/6cm    Box: W/11.2cm, H/4.8cm*

The bottle is colored porcelain glaze made into the "elephant of peace" pattern. The Chinese word for elephant sounds like the word for auspiciousness, so the elephant is a traditional auspicious symbol. Many decorations use the elephant pattern, and the "elephant of peace" pattern shows an elephant with a treasure vase on its back. The treasure vase contains holy water that can bring good fortune to the people, and it symbolizes peace on earth.

The workmanship of this snuff bottle is refined, and the inscription on the bottom says it was made during the reign of Qianlong. Accompanied by a red lacquer box, it is both noble and graceful.

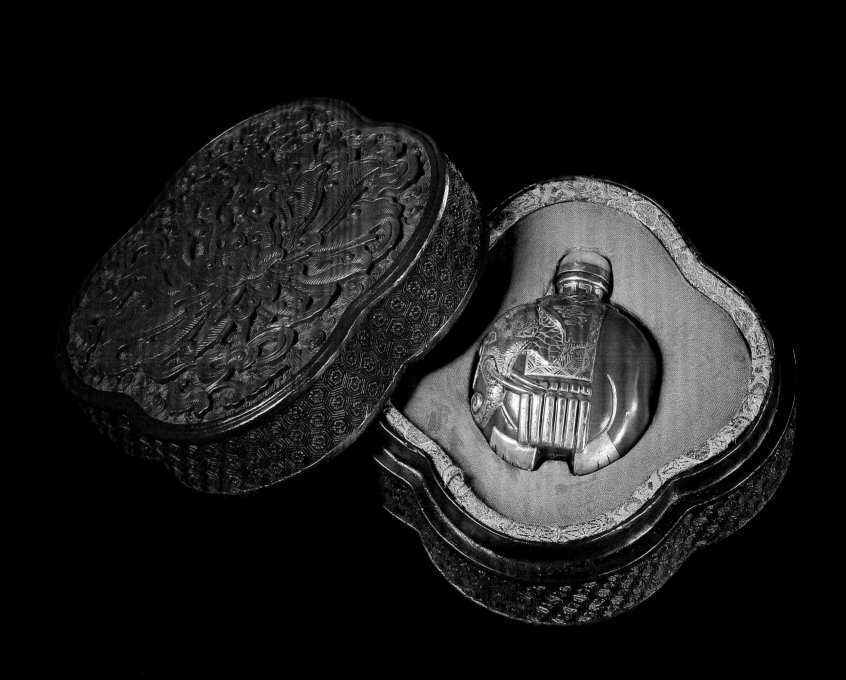

# 圖說作者

## Bamboo and Wood Carving

| | |
|---|---|
| Ming Dynasty  Bamboo carving scholars under a pine tree brush holder, Gu Jue signature | Chen Yung-Cheng |
| Qing Dynasty  Bamboo carving light boat skimming past ten thousand sombre crags brush holder, Xi Huang signature | Chen Yung-Cheng |
| Qing Dynasty  Bamboo carving Guanyin seated statue | Tsai Yao-Ching |
| Qing Dynasty  Bamboo carving, Xiao Song signature, "the fisherman profits" | Tsai Yao-Ching |
| Qing Dynasty  Bamboo carving human figure | Tsai Yao-Ching |
| Qing Dynasty  Bamboo root God of longevity | Tsai Yao-Ching |
| Qing Dynasty  Bamboo carving phoenix presents beneficence | Chen Yung-Cheng |
| Ming Dynasty  Wanli Era  Red sandalwood incense tray | Chen Yung-Cheng |
| Qing Dynasty  Red sandalwood cloud and dragon pattern imperial seal box | Chen Yung-Cheng |
| Qing Dynasty  Red sandalwood cloud and dragon pattern square box | Chen Yung-Cheng |
| Qing Dynasty  Red sandalwood  "Han-tao" curio cabinet | Chen Yung-Cheng |
| Qing Dynasty  Red sandalwood seawater cloud and dragon pattern brush holder | Chen Yung-Cheng |
| Qing Dynasty  Boxwood carving human figures | Chen Yung-Cheng |

## Nobility and Refinement

| | |
|---|---|
| Qing Dynasty Yongzheng Era  "Standing Portrait of Emperor Yongzheng  in Court Robes" Ink and color on paper | Wang Hsin-Kong |
| Yuan Dynasty  Yuan embroidery painting of the four joys of early spring | Huang Chun Hsiu |
| Qing Dynasty  Qianlong Era  "Ascending Mount Tai" scroll with imperial poetry | Tsai Yao-Ching |
| Qing Dynasty  Zhang Ruo-Ai's copy of Tang Dynasty peony branch painting | Tsai Yao-Ching |
| Qing Dynasty  Red lacquer "Returning from battle in triumph" rounded plaque | Huang Chun Hsiu |
| Ming Dyansty  Temple wall painting  Fragment of Female Celestial Presenting Treasure | Wang Hsin-Kong |
| Ming Dynasty  Yongle Era  Gilt bronze Avalokitesvara | Yang Shih-Chao |
| Ming Dynasty  Gilt bronze four-armed Manjusri Bodhisattva | Yang Shih-Chao |
| Ming Dynasty  Bronze Zhou sacrificial animal with gold and silver inlay | Yang Shih-Chao |
| Qing Dynasty  Gilt bronze double phoenix censer stand | Yang Shih-Chao |
| Qing Dynasty  Bronze gold-splashed tripod burner | Yang Shih-Chao |
| Qing Dynasty  Qianlong Era  "Liao" glass teat-shaped foot tripod censer, inscribed as made during the reign of Qianlong | Chen Yung-Cheng |
| Qing Dynasty  Imperial Qianlong crystal medicine bottle | Tsai Yao-Ching |
| Qing Dynasty  Qianlong Era  Coral red glaze painted gold snuff bottle wit red lacquer box, inscribed as made during the reign of Qianlong | Tsai Yao-Ching |

# Commentator

## Tianhuang

Qing Dynasty  Tianhuang beast body square seal  Inscription: Huang Zi Shu Yin                                     Yang Shih-Chao

Qing Dynasty  Tianhuang beast body square seal  Inscription: Le Yi Tang Tu Shu Ji                                  Yang Shih-Chao

Qing Dynasty  Tianhuang evil-averting beast paperweight  Yu Xuan signature                                        Yang Shih-Chao

Qing Dynasty  Tianhuangdong dragon tiger square seal  Inscription: Yan Po Jiang Shang                              Yang Shih-Chao

Qing Dynasty  Tianhuang evil-averting body square seal                                                            Yang Shih-Chao

Qing Dynasty  Tianhuang intricate relief carving square seal                                                      Yang Shih-Chao

Qing Dynasty  Tianhuang tile body square seal                                                                     Yang Shih-Chao

Qing Dynasty  Tianhuang evil-averting body square seal                                                            Yang Shih-Chao

Qing Dynasty  Tianhuang evil-averting body square seal                                                            Yang Shih-Chao

Qing Dynasty  Black skin Tianhuang intricate relief carving irregular shape seal                                  Yang Shih-Chao

Qing Dynasty  Tianhuang natural shape seal                                                                        Yang Shih-Chao

Qing Dynasty  White hibiscus square seal  Shang Jun signature                                                     Yang Shih-Chao

Qing Dynasty  White hibiscus flat body flying horse pattern square seal  Inscription: Zhang Jia Yin               Yang Shih-Chao

Qing Dynasty  Hibiscus flat top flying bird pattern square seal                                                   Yang Shih-Chao

Qing Dynasty  Duling stone flat top pair of square seals                                                          Yang Shih-Chao

Qing Dynasty  Qingtian tile body square seal                                                                      Yang Shih-Chao

## Rhino Horn Carvings

Ming Dynasty  Rhino horn carving Guanyin seated statue                                                            Tsai Yao-Ching

Ming Dynasty  Rhino horn carving bean pod small cup                                                               Tsai Yao-Ching

Qing Dynasty  Rhino horn carving hornless dragon pattern small cup                                                Tsai Yao-Ching

Qing Dynasty  Rhino horn carving flowers small cup                                                                Tsai Yao-Ching

# 所寶惟賢——爽伯文物鑑賞

發行人
黃永川

出版者
國立歷史博物館
地址：一○○臺北市南海路四十九號
電話：+886-2-23610270
傳真：+886-2-23610171
網站：www.nmh.gov.tw

編輯
國立歷史博物館編輯委員會

執行總監
吳宗明

主編
戈思明

執行編輯
王慧珍　宋建興

美術設計
凱嵐視覺傳達
地址：上海市宜昌路七五一號 B 二○三室
電話：+86-21-51752728

美編顧問
王行恭

文字校正
黃靖雅

英文翻譯
萬象翻譯股份有限公司

英文審稿
邱勢浲

英文校閱
陳嘉翎

作品攝影
林憲煜

總務
許志榮

會計
劉瑩珠

展售處
國立歷史博物館文化服務處
地址：一○○臺北市南海路四十九號
電話：+886-2-23610270

國家書店松江門市
地址：一○四臺北市松江路二○九號一樓
電話：+886-2-25180207

國家網路書店
http://www.govbooks.com.tw

製版印刷
上海大誠印刷有限公司
地址：上海市真北路三一九弄五號
電話：+86-21-62503311

著作財產權人
國立歷史博物館
吳先旺

版次
初版

出版日期
中華民國九十七年十一月（精裝）

定價
新台幣 八○○○元（全套三冊）

統一編號
1009702519

國際書號
978-986-01-5491-7

◎本書保留所有權利

欲利用本書全部或部分內容者，需徵求著作
人及著作財產權人同意或書面授權。
請洽展覽組（電話：+886-2-23610270）

五洲製藥股份有限公司
地址：一○四臺北市中山區
明水路三八七號
電話：+886-2-25333911
傳真：+886-2-25334611

國家圖書館出版品預行編目資料

所寶惟賢：爽伯文物鑑賞
＝ A Sage's respect for artistic treasures:
Collection of Uncle Shuang
/國立歷史博物館編委會編輯—初版
—臺北市：史博館，民97.11
　　面；　　公分

ISBN 978-986-01-5491-7（精裝）

1. 玉器　2. 古器物　3. 圖錄

794.4025　　　　　　　　97018478

# A Sage's Respect for Artistic Treasures
## — Collection of Uncle Shuang

**Publisher**
Huang Yung-Chuan

**Commissioner**
National Museum of History
Address: 49 Nan-Hai Road, Taipei 100, Taiwan
Tel: +886-2-23610270
Fax: +886-2-23610171
http: www.nmh.gov.tw

U.C.Pharma
Address: 387 Mean-Sway Road, Taipei 104, Taiwan
Tel: +886-2-25339911
Fax: +886-2-25334611

**Coordinator**
Wu Chung-Ming

**Editorial Committee**
Editor Committee of National Museum of History

**Chief Editor**
Jeff Ge

**Executive Editor**
Wang Hui-Jen, Soong Chien-Hsin

**Graphic Designer**
KRW Visual Communication
Address: B203, 751 Yi-Chang Road, Shanghai, China
Tel: +86-21-51752728

**Art Consultant**
David Wang

**Contents Proofreader**
Huang Ching-Ya

**English Translator**
Linguitronics Co., Ltd.

**English Proofreader**
Mark Rawson

**English Review**
Chen Jia-Lin

**Photographer**
Lin Shen-Yu

**Chief General Affairs**
Hsu Chin-Jung

**Chief Accountant**
Liu Ying-Chu

**Printing**
SHANGHAI DAH CHEN PRINTING CO.,LTD
Address: No.5, Alley 3199, Zhenbei Rd.,Shanghai, 200333, China
Tel: +86-21-62503311

**Publication Dates**
November 2008 (Hard Cover)

**Edition**
First Edition

**Price**
NT$ 8,000  (A set with three volumes)

**Gift Shop**
Cultural Service Department of National Museum of History
Address: 49 Nan-Hai Rd., Taipei 100, Taiwan
Tel: +886-2-23610270

Government Publications Bookstore
Address: 1F, No.209, Sung Chiang Rd., Taipei 104, Taiwan
Tel:+886-2-25180207

Government Online Bookstore
http://www.govbooks.com.tw

**GPN**
1009702519

**ISBN**
978-986-01-5491-7

GNP    1009702519
定價    NT$ 8,000